**seven steps
to starting
and running
an editorial
consulting business**

Seven Steps to Starting and Running an Editorial Consulting Business

Jane M. Frutchey

Unlimited Publishing
Bloomington, Indiana

Copyright © 2001 by Jane M. Frutchey

Distributing Publisher:
Unlimited Publishing, LLC
Bloomington, Indiana

http://www.unlimitedpublishing.com

Cover and Book Design by Charles King
Copyright © 2001 by Unlimited Publishing, LLC
This book was typeset with Adobe® InDesign®, using the Myriad® and Minion® typefaces.

All rights reserved under Title 17, U.S. Code, International and Pan-American Copyright Conventions. No part of this work may be reproduced or transmitted in any form or by any means, electronic or mechanical, including photocopying, scanning, recording or duplication by any information storage or retrieval system without prior written permission from the author(s) and publisher(s), except for the inclusion of brief quotations with attribution in a review or report. Requests for permission or further information should be addressed to the author(s).

Unlimited Publishing LLC provides worldwide book design, printing, marketing and distribution services for professional writers and small to mid-size presses, serving as distributing publisher. Sole responsibility for the content of each work rests with the author(s) and/or contributing publisher(s). The opinions expressed herein may not be interpreted in any way as representing those of Unlimited Publishing, nor any of its affiliates.

Copies of this book and others
are available to order online, anytime at:

http://www.unlimitedpublishing.com/authors

ISBN 1-58832-040-5

Unlimited Publishing
Bloomington, Indiana

To all of my voices of encouragement, past and present: Sr. Ann Gabriel, S.S.J.; Mary Cary; Patricia Novak; Michael Poletynski; Dr. Richard Vatz; Dr. Carolyn Hill; Dr. Harvey Lillywhite; Dr. Linda Mahin; and especially, Dr. Linda Meade.

Special thanks to Mr. Trumbull Rogers, fellow editor, for assisting with current statistics on editorial freelancers.

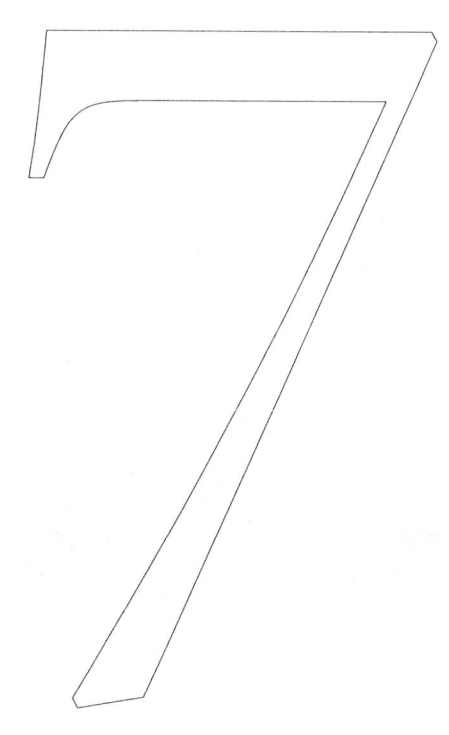

Contents

Preface / xi

Introduction / xv

Step 1: Consider the Practicalities of Self-Employment / 1
Do I Have the Traits Necessary for Self-Employment? / 2
Do I Have Enough Education and Work Experience? / 4
When Is the Optimal Time to Leave My Full-Time Job? / 14
Have I Read Enough Background Material about
   Starting and Operating a Home-Based Business? / 16
Have I Considered the Advantages and
   Disadvantages of a Home-Based Business? / 18
Have I Saved Enough Money for Start-Up? / 27

Step 2: Take a How-To Course or Seminar and Seek Free Advice / 29
Small Business Administration / 30
Chamber of Commerce / 31
National Association of Home-Based Businesses / 32
Community Colleges / 33
Consultants and Freelancers / 33

Step 3: Contact Professional Organizations / 37
Benefits to Joining an Organization / 38
Questions to Ask When Evaluating an Organization / 40
Caveats to Joining an Organization / 43

Step 4: Find a Qualified Certified Public Accountant / 45
    Setting Up Your Business / 46
    Opening Bank Accounts for Your Business / 47
    Tracking Business Expenses and Income / 48
    Making Quarterly Estimated Tax Payments / 49
    Handling Tax-Related Paperwork and Other Matters / 51

Step 5: Consider the Practicalities of Running Your Home Office / 55
    Setting Your Fees / 56
    Establishing Your Work Space / 63
    Purchasing Office Furniture, Equipment, and Supplies / 65
    Financing Your Start-Up Expenses / 71
    Confronting Unexpected Disasters / 73
    Dealing with Nonpaying Clients / 78
    Dealing with Rush Assignments / 79
    Dealing with Conflicting Client Obligations / 82
    Dealing with Burnout / 86

Step 6: Cultivating and Maintaining Your Client Base / 91
    Never Burn Bridges / 91
    Win Word-of-Mouth Referrals / 94
    Make Some Cold Calls / 95
    Take a Test / 98
    Prepare a Simple, Informative Marketing Packet / 99
    List Your Business in a Directory or Database / 103
    Experiment with Paid Advertising / 104
    Experiment with Free Publicity / 107
    Written Contracts and Verbal Agreements / 110

Step 7: Keep Your Business Running Smoothly in the Years Ahead / 113
Do a Meticulous Job / 113
Stay in Touch with Clients / 117
Pay Your Taxes on Time / 118
Chart a Course for Success / 119

Afterword / 121

Suggested Readings / 123

Appendix A: Marketing Packet / 125
Business Card Sample / 125
Brochure Sample / 126
Flier Sample / 128
Resumé Sample / 129

Appendix B: Resources for Editors / 131
Books / 131
Grammar Hotlines / 134
Periodicals / 135
Professional Organizations / 137
Websites / 139

Index / 141

Feedback or Questions / 145

Preface

I remember clearly my last day of full-time editorial employment: a bright autumn day, with azure skies, puffy white clouds, and temperature in the 70s. The birds were singing, and to me, it seemed they sang louder that day. During my last few hours as a "captive" employee, I said goodbye to my co-workers, turned in my I.D. badge, and ran to my car. I threw a box of my office-related possessions in the trunk, kicked off my high-heeled pumps, took off my business suit jacket, got in my car, and never looked back. A huge smile was plastered across my face as I turned up the radio, screamed "Yippee," and drove away from my now-former-employer's parking lot. As excited as I was about my new endeavor as an independent editorial consultant, I was also scared of the unknown. Beneath the ecstasy of leaving behind the 9-to-5 corporate world lurked anxiety and fear about forging ahead on my own. After all, I had never run a business before, so how could I be sure I could make it as an independent editor?

Although I was unsure of what I would confront in the months and years to come, I was certain of one thing: I had the desire to succeed as an independent editor. And so, by the time my full-time editorial job with a multimillion-dollar government contractor became absolutely unbearable, I already had begun the task of feverishly conducting my research. I read and skimmed dozens of books, magazines, and newsletter articles, and I interviewed and spoke with other consultants and freelance editors.

When I began my research into this exciting opportunity, I scanned or read multiple references in their entirety. There was no single source that compiled all the answers to the questions that I had related to the practicalities of starting and running my business. The steps outlined in this book are the ones that I took and pursued to start and run my editorial consulting business successfully for more than a decade. I hope to continue on this path, running my own home-based business for many more decades to come. I also hope to impart to you the knowledge that I have acquired along the way so that you may experience your own successes and avoid some of the same mistakes I made early on in my business.

When I began my business, I had about seven years of editorial experience, which I had acquired in the corporate and nonprofit communications environments, as well as in the public relations/advertising agency setting. I kept in touch with many of my colleagues and former co-workers who held jobs in the communications field. I initially planned to pursue corporate clients because I had no experience editing books, but I was curious about, and interested in, that type of editing as well. I was confident in my skills as an editor, and I wanted to pursue new opportunities and gain additional experience working with book publishers.

Through networking with my friends and colleagues, I found three clients before I left my full-time editorial job: a local business newspaper, a nonprofit organization, and a small financial institution. I also had submitted my resume to several book publishers with a cover letter explaining my interest in editorial work. A local book publisher contacted me shortly thereafter, and sent me a copyediting test, which I immediately completed and returned within the week. Within two weeks, I heard back from that publisher and received my first book-editing assignment, and I knew, then, that I happily would be relinquishing my full-time employee status. After that fourth contact, I knew I had enough work to fill my schedule. I was officially on my way to starting and running my own editing business.

If you have ever dreamed of relinquishing the rigors of your full-time job as a staff editor, one of the most exciting opportunities awaits you as you become your own boss and independent consulting editor. As a staff editor, you may yearn to make it on your own and pursue your own home-based business once you have gained adequate experience and a well-rounded editorial background. Starting and running your own editorial consulting business offers many attractive advantages if you are diligent, persistent, hard working, and prepared to make the transition from working in a more structured 9-to-5 atmosphere to working for yourself in a more relaxed environment—your own home-based office.

Breaking away from the full-time employee routine can pave the way to opportunities that an inflexible corporate environment cannot provide, such as the abilities to be your own boss, set your own pay scale, select your work assignments, and work more convenient hours that suit your personal schedule.

If you have a variety of editorial skills and experiences, can thoroughly research the market and target a niche where your skills fit in, and are prepared to be a persistent salesperson and marketer of your services, you will successfully launch and maintain your editorial consulting business. I am confident that you, too, can apply the seven steps described in this book and find your own way to success. You may follow each of these steps with the intention of pursuing a particular type of editing and later discover, as I did, that your business is unfolding in an entirely new and different direction. And therein lies the excitement. New opportunities, challenges, and skills, and a variety of editorial projects, are just ahead. It's up to you to go into that uncharted territory, if you dare, and discover those hidden treasures that come with starting and running your own business. Along the way, you might even uncover your own Hope diamond—one-of-a-kind editorial expertise that only you can provide your clients. Mine that expertise, refine it, and share it with others. No doubt, you'll soon find that your clients return again and again, consulting you for that expertise.

In this book, I do not explain the mechanics or minutiae of editing; there are several excellent books available to you if you need practice in, or a review of, both developmental editing and copyediting (see Suggested Readings). I have focused instead on the step-by-step process you will take in order to get your editorial consulting business started and to keep it running smoothly for many years to come.

I hope this book enlightens you and proves to be a helpful guide as you start your business and watch it steadily grow in the years to come. My greatest desire is that you will refer to the information, tips, and case examples presented in this book many times throughout the course of your business' start-up and growth. I extend my best wishes to you for your success as you make the transformation from a full-time employee working for someone else to an independent home-based business owner.

Introduction

In starting a home-based venture—and in undertaking practically any new endeavor—there always is some good news and inevitably some bad news to share. And so, I'll begin with some good news about editorial consulting in the new millennium. According to Paul and Sarah Edwards, self-employment experts and authors of *The Best Home Businesses for the 21st Century*, there are more than 20,000 book publishers in the United States and another 20,000 or so periodicals publishers, not to mention the numerous small, mid-size, and large corporations throughout our country. The good news for those considering the possibility of breaking free from the rigors of their 9-to-5 editorial jobs is that the overwhelming majority of all these publishers and corporations are small to mid-size; therefore, they rely heavily on professional assistance from independent editorial contractors and consultants.

The Board of Directors of the Editorial Freelancers Association (EFA) estimates that there are approximately 10,000 freelance or independent editors in the United States and about half as many abroad. This tally is an informal estimate because the majority of these freelancers who provide editorial services have home-based operations and there is no central registry for home-based editors. However, according to both the EFA and the U.S. Department of Labor, Bureau of Labor Statistics, the number of editorial freelancers has increased steadily over the course of the 1990s and into the 21st century, and the job outlook for independent editors is excellent in the years ahead as the need for the services of independent editors continues to rise. A whirlwind of mergers in traditional publishing houses, leading to downsizing—along with the ubiquity of electronic publishing, desktop publishing, and the ever-growing numbers of small and mid-size for-profit and nonprofit businesses overall—is no doubt contributing to this increased need. The future, then, for editorial consultants seems to be brimming with opportunity as greater numbers of publishers, both traditional and corporate or custom, outsource their editorial services, including developmental editing, copyediting, proofreading, and indexing.

Based on my experience running my own editorial consulting business for more than 10 years, as well as on my reading to keep informed about current trends in the field and job forecasts released by the Bureau of Labor Statistics, some of the best opportunities for editorial consultants to use their skills exist in the following fields:

- *Business communications*—In all types of business, there is an ongoing need for assistance with advertising, marketing, public relations, and employee communications efforts. There is a need for assistance with in-house training programs held for employees, as well as the need for writing and editorial assistance with the specialized training manuals produced and used for those in-house programs.

- *Health care*—The health care field teems with new discoveries and information each year. Publishers of scholarly texts and journals need editorial services of all kinds, especially for publications targeted to the allied health care professions, including dentistry, medicine, nursing, psychiatry, psychology, veterinary medicine, and so on. These types of publishers produce volumes of pertinent, up-to-date health care–related information. Although some of this information is published in standard bound book or journal format, other works are published as CD ROMS, audiocassettes, or videocassettes. In addition, the public relations or marketing departments of some hospitals, elder care facilities, and health maintenance organizations use the services of editorial consultants.

- *Law*—We live in a litigious society, and that fact translates to opportunity for the editorial consultant interested in assisting lawyers by digesting or editing and formatting lengthy depositions and other legal documents.

- *Technical* or *multimedia*—With the advent of high-tech computerized equipment of all sorts, there is a growing need for writers and editors who can assist with the multitude of software and hardware training manuals that must accompany the equipment. There is also a growing demand for World Wide Web page designers and website writers and editors. The vast amount of information presented on the Internet in the form of electronic magazines and books (e-zines and e-books) further increases the demand for editors with specialized skills in these areas.

In addition to the opportunities available in the aforementioned fields, there seems to be a widespread need for temporary on-site editorial assistance. The editorial consultant who thrives on variety and travel could make a nice living hiring his or her services out on a temporary on-site basis. There is a definitive need for on-site assistance because of corporate downsizing efforts and because some departments inevitably become short-staffed due to extended vacations, medical or maternity leave, and employees' moving into new positions within the company or their leaving the company to accept a new position.

As an editorial consultant, you will have the chance to work on a wide variety of writing and editing assignments, covering a vast array of topics and subject matter. This is just one of the perquisites you'll experience while running your own business:

you can pick and choose the assignments presented to you that you'd like to work on most. One week you may be coordinating a corporate newsletter or magazine; the next, copyediting a nonfiction how-to book on gardening or a work of fiction, such as a thriller. Because you'll be running your own business and selecting your editorial assignments, the field is wide open to you.

And now for the bad news: Although there is a wealth of opportunity available for the hardworking, persistent editorial consultant, the U.S. Small Business Administration estimates that more than 50% of all home-based businesses fail within the first five years of start-up. Those failures largely can be attributed to five factors:

1. Poor planning

2. Inadequate marketing/promotional efforts

3. Failure to develop and expand client contacts

4. Failure to follow up or stay in touch with clients

5. Failure to do a thorough job that meets clients' needs

I am living proof that you indeed can beat the odds and see your business grow and succeed beyond the five-year mark. With hard work and persistence, your business will thrive, too.

To help you avoid the five factors that contribute to a business' premature failure, I have included in this book some journaling exercises, case examples, and tips that will prove helpful to you as you set up and run your business.

Chapter 1 leads readers through a complete self-assessment of personality traits, education, work experience, and skills through interactive journaling opportunities. Questions are posed to aid you in thoroughly evaluating and considering the traits and experience necessary to run a home-based consulting business. Case examples in this chapter will enrich your understanding of the more practical issues and challenges confronting the editorial consultant at start-up. Chapter 1 also helps you determine the optimal time for leaving full-time employment behind so that you may start your home-based business, helps you evaluate the advantages and disadvantages of running a home-based business, and helps you assess your current financial status at your business' start-up.

Chapter 2 informs you about sources from which you can obtain helpful introductory information for business start-up and success. You will learn about courses and seminars offered by the U.S. Small Business Administration, U.S. Chamber of Commerce, National Association of Home-Based Businesses, and local community colleges. You will also discover that there are opportunities for networking with, and seeking free advice and guidance from, other consultants and independent contractors who are currently doing the work that you might like to do.

Chapter 3 covers professional organizations that are available to assist independent editors or consultants. This chapter is a discussion of the benefits editorial consultants will receive by joining one or more of these organizations, including networking opportunities, listings in membership directories, job hotlines, and arbitration services that help editorial consultants negotiate with nonpaying clients. By reading this chapter, you will learn how to evaluate more carefully these organizations to determine which ones will provide you with the most services, support, and value for your hard-earned new-business dollars.

In Chapter 4, I explain why editorial consultants must find and enlist the services of a professional certified public accountant (CPA) who can help at business start-up and during the years ahead. The counsel of a professional accountant is necessary from the outset, when you are planning and starting your business. Your CPA will help you understand the process of making quarterly estimated tax payments, as well as explain the end-of-year business tax return and itemized deductions. If you have a CPA assisting you, you'll be relieved of the additional burdens of filing important tax-related paperwork and handling other tax matters that arise during the lifetime of your business. In this chapter, you also will find pointers on the best way to keep track of all of your business expenses and income.

In Chapter 5, I review the numerous practical considerations in running a home-based business, including setting fees; establishing a work space; determining start-up expenses for furniture, equipment, and supplies, as well as the means for financing them; handling unexpected disasters, especially technical problems with office equipment; and facing everyday challenges such as nonpaying clients, rush assignments, conflicting client obligations, and burnout. Chapter 5 also includes a formula for calculating minimum hourly fees, and checklists for essential office equipment and supplies.

Chapter 6 guides readers in the most effective methods for cultivating and maintaining a core group of clients. In this chapter, I discuss networking and winning word-of-mouth referrals, making cold telephone calls, taking tests, preparing and distributing marketing packets, listing your professional services in membership directories, experimenting with low-cost advertising and free publicity, and establishing a presence on the World Wide Web. This chapter also briefly reviews written contracts and verbal agreements.

Chapter 7 summarizes and reiterates the three most important principles that you, as an editorial consultant, must bear in mind in order to start your business and see it thrive in years to come: always do a meticulous job, always stay in touch with your clients, and always pay your taxes on time.

For your reference, I've also included Suggested Readings and two Appendixes. Appendix A shows an example of materials that you may want to include in your marketing packet, such as a consultant's resume, brochure, flier, and business card.

Appendix B is a list of helpful resources for editors, including books, grammar hotlines, periodicals, professional organizations, and websites.

Chapter 1

Step 1: Consider the Practicalities of Self-Employment

$\mathcal{S}$tarting your own business requires a tremendous amount of soul-searching and thoughtful contemplation about several practical but critical issues. A thorough self-assessment that includes taking stock of your personality traits, education, and work experience is an essential starting point in establishing your editorial consulting business. Other preliminary considerations are the vast market from which you will cultivate your clientele and the optimal time to leave your full-time position so that you may focus on your newly established consulting business. Research is important as you develop your business plan, so you'll want to review as much information as possible about starting and operating your own business for helpful suggestions and guidance. Furthermore, you must evaluate the advantages and disadvantages of running a home-based business to appreciate more completely the challenges you'll face and commitments you'll make as you undertake your venture. A final matter for consideration is your current financial status, to determine what you realistically can afford to spend at your business' start-up.

As you take the initial step in starting your editorial consulting business, I recommend keeping a business start-up journal. Your start-up journal simply can be a spiralbound notebook, for recording your thoughts, ideas, and plans about start-up. Note taking in the journal will keep you organized as you proceed through each step of the start-up process detailed in this book. Just getting your thoughts on paper may help you to think more clearly and stay motivated about your hopes for accomplishment and success. Your business start-up journal could help you work through some of the fears and concerns you may have about being self-employed.

Do I Have the Traits Necessary for Self-Employment?

I have discovered 10 essential personality traits you'll need in order to start and run your own editorial consulting business and ensure its success. Documenting your thoughts in your business start-up journal as you read through the following statements may aid in your self-assessment and commitment to starting your business.

1. *I enjoy working alone.* As a consultant or an independent contractor, you can become quite lonely. If you're the type of person who enjoys office camaraderie and thrives in a work atmosphere where there are lots of people around, being on your own can pose a major psychological adjustment.

2. *I am self-disciplined and self-motivated.* Remember that when you work for yourself, there are no higher-ups watching over you, telling you what to do, or handing you assignments. You must have the discipline and motivation to work a full day, each day, and to obtain a full workload to keep you busy and financially stable.

3. *I enjoy multiple responsibilities.* Not only will you be the owner of your editorial consulting business, but you also

will be business manager; chief financial officer; secretary; public relations, marketing, and advertising representative; account executive; office supply clerk; and courier.

4. *I am willing to work long hours.* You will have to sacrifice your personal time—weekends, holidays, and special family occasions included—and work long hours at the start-up of your business. However, those sacrifices will ease once your business is well established.

5. *I am persistent.* You will need plenty of persistence and "stick-to-itiveness" when you are just starting your business, especially when cultivating your core group of clients and soliciting work assignments.

6. *I am detail oriented.* To excel in your editorial consulting business, you'll need a keen eye for detail in your day-to-day work tasks. To keep your business going and growing in the years to come, you'll have to do not just a *good* job but a *meticulous* job.

7. *I am good at problem solving.* Not only must you possess well-rounded editorial skills, but you also must be adept at, and comfortable with, pointing out problems to your clients and offering alternative effective solutions. Your services will be of more value if you can help clients troubleshoot and problem solve complex editorial projects.

8. *I am highly organized.* As a consultant, you will be juggling a multitude of business-related responsibilities in addition to your hands-on editorial tasks. Being a business owner with numerous business-related deadlines and being an editor with multiple client deadlines can be an overwhelming balancing act. Excellent organizational skills will prevent you from faltering.

9. *I am an effective planner.* Contemplate your business plan well in advance of start-up. Have definite ideas about what you would like to accomplish, which clients you would like to work with, and how you can make your business grow in the future.

10. *I am willing to take risks with my finances.* Financial matters can be a bit uncertain when you are just beginning your consulting business. During the start-up years, you won't be able to determine how much you'll earn from one year to the next and how much expendable funds you'll have available. You should have enough money saved in advance of your business start-up to carry you through at least four to six months without income.

If you agree that all or most of the 10 previous statements describe you, then indeed, you are an excellent candidate for an independent editorial consultant. And, in my experience, most editorial consultants would describe themselves as possessing the majority of the aforementioned characteristics.

Do I Have Enough Education and Work Experience?

Education and work experience are both important factors to consider before you begin your own consulting business. As an editorial consultant, you could probably get by with at least a bachelor's degree, but I'm a firm believer that a master's degree is much more helpful and will give you a leading edge over your competitors. If you will be working with clients such as scholarly books publishers, teaching hospitals, and some of the more high-tech electronics or telecommunications industries, for example, I believe a master's degree is absolutely essential. Otherwise, you are likely to become lost or overwhelmed by the industry jargon, acronyms, abbreviations, and detailed stylistic preferences that are relevant to your clients. I doubt that I would be an editorial consultant today if I had only a bachelor's degree. I believe my language and editorial skills were greatly refined and enhanced through completing a master's degree program in professional writing.

If you do not have an advanced degree in writing, business communications, or mass communication, I strongly encourage concurrent graduate-level study at business start-up, or perhaps you could obtain a graduate degree *before* starting your consulting business. I worked toward my master's degree simultaneously at the start-up of my business. At that time, my business was a part-time effort so that I also could focus on my graduate studies but have an income to assist with my tuition and fees. Upon graduation, I was armed with advanced writing, editing, and research skills, and I was better prepared to serve my clients when I increased my workload to full-time capacity.

Before venturing out on your own as an editorial consultant, I recommend acquiring as much editorial and communications experience as possible. At least five years' experience as a full-time writer, editor, publications coordinator, or public relations/communications assistant is essential. Another two to three more years in a full-time position would greatly benefit your business management skills so that you are well prepared to meet and overcome business-related challenges once you are on your own.

The editorial skills that you'll need to succeed as a consultant are numerous and diverse. I once attended a seminar on mass communication trends and one of the speakers advised, "Practitioners in the communications field should not be specialists; they should be generalists." I believe that this piece of advice applies to editorial consultants as well. You can be a specialist in certain fields that are of interest to you, such as health care or law, but be a generalist in your communication and editorial skills because you will be able to offer your clients so much more. The more skills you have and the more varied your background, the more valuable you will be to your clients.

You can assess just how well rounded your experience and skills are by asking yourself the questions that follow. Keep track of your responses to, and thoughts on, these questions in your business start-up journal to help identify which skills and experiences you may lack or need to improve.

- Do I have experience in newspaper or magazine journalism?

- Do I have experience in books or journals publishing?

- Do I have experience in advertising or public relations?

- Do I have experience in corporate communications?

- Do I have experience in nonprofit communications?

- Do I have the following essential editorial skills:

  - Analyzing data?

  - Copyediting and line editing?

  - Critiquing?

  - Design and layout?

  - Fact-checking?

  - Interviewing?

- Photography?

- Proofreading?

- Publications coordinating?

- Writing?

- Do I have impeccable language skills?

- Do I know the rules regarding proper language mechanics, including spelling, grammar, punctuation, capitalization, word usage, syntax, and terminology?

- Do I have a critical eye for analyzing facts and statistics?

- Am I able to analyze others' writing and recognize illogical organization, unclear passages, and poor transitions?

- Am I able to recognize rhetorical errors such as biases, faulty reasoning, sweeping generalizations, contradictory statements, redundancies, ambiguities, libelous statements, and incorrect or outdated facts?

In my years as an editorial consultant, I have seen a tremendous amount of poor, unclear, and disorganized writing—in the business world and among academia. It seems to me that the worst perpetrators of language abuse are those with MBAs, PhDs, and MDs—those who are highly intelligent and should know how to construct a comprehensible, organized paragraph. Perhaps it is laziness or maybe time constraints that impose roadblocks to the writing and language skills of the intelligentsia. Whatever the reason, there are definitely individuals and organizations out there in dire need of editorial assistance. If you possess all or most of the skills and experience previously listed, or if you are willing to acquire them, you can become indispensable to those who need your services, knowledge, and expertise and do not have the time to tinker with their writing projects.

Case Example 1

After I had completed the editing of my first book manuscript for one local editor and returned it to him, he called me early the next day and asked where I had received my editorial training.

"My training comes from a combination of sources," I informed him. "In Catholic elementary school, I diagrammed sentences at an early age, and I did so again in a high school honors English class. I had the good fortune of working with a former book editor in one of my full-time positions, and I absorbed a lot of information from her. I also recently completed a master's degree in professional writing."

"Well," he said, "I've never worked with an editor whose skills were so highly refined. You have a real gift for improving and making sense of what these authors are trying to say."

As an editorial consultant, you may not receive much positive, encouraging feedback from all of your clients on a daily basis; however, when you do, it will be a tremendous boost to your self-esteem. Know that your language skills and knowledge are valued and may even be recognized by your clients, especially those who truly appreciate a job well done.

Case Example 2

One former client requested that I edit and coordinate all revisions for a document that was being prepared for an upcoming congressional session. The document was to be distributed to hundreds of congressional representatives. I reviewed the first draft, correcting spelling, grammar, and punctuation errors and pointing out stylistic inconsistencies, unclear and ambiguous passages, and organizational problems within this multiauthor document. I had queried the lead author with suggestions for improving the clarity and organization of the document's contents, but the author did not want to change the text. Grammatical errors, lack of transitions, and poor organization greatly detracted from the clarity of the document.

When I initially met with the client to discuss the editorial approach to take with this document, the client's directions were to "polish it to perfection." As with any job that I undertake, I did as the client requested and assessed the document for basic errors in language mechanics. I thoroughly evaluated the material for clarity, organization, and consistency in stylistics and terminology. At one of the many subsequent meetings to discuss revisions, the client turned to me and said, "You've done a thorough job, but we really are not concerned about proper grammar, syntax, and organization. The content is what matters."

In my view, the clarity of the content relies heavily upon proper language mechanics, organization, and stylistic consistency. When the client made what to me was an uninformed statement, I knew I was definitely not accepting any future assignments from that organization. I do not do any editorial job halfway, and I will not compromise my professionalism by doing so.

In some instances, the customer or client is not always right. Editing requires highly specialized language skills and experience of which the average writer is not often aware or informed. You will have to decide how willing, under certain circumstances, you will be either to sacrifice or uphold your professionalism as an editorial consultant. Will you let some errors go for the sake of appeasing your client, or will you do your job accurately and thoroughly, trying to persuade a client to accept your professional standpoint?

Impeccable language skills are the sine qua non for the editorial consultant. You may consider your current language skills to be perfectly acceptable for doing business as an editorial consultant. However, there is a decided difference between the consultant who does a good job and one who does a meticulous job. You must always strive to do a meticulous job for all of your clients, and that means improving on the skills you already possess. How do you go about improving your language skills? There are several simple exercises you can try so that your brain cells receive a vigorous daily workout.

- Read everything and take it apart, word by word. Analyze memos, junk mail, articles, newsletters, books, short stories—anything and everything that contains the written word. Read widely and always ask yourself, How would I improve this piece of writing?

- Study the parts of speech, brush up on your grammar and punctuation rules, and practice diagramming sentences or learn how to diagram them if you've never done so. In diagramming sentences, you will acquire invaluable skills in identifying parts of speech, explaining how each word functions in a sentence, and in turn, explaining to your clients why certain word choices are inappropriate in a particular piece of writing. I am not certain if diagramming sentences is still taught in schools or colleges today (my guess is that it is not, as indicated by much of the writing I review and edit). If diagramming sentences is a lost skill, I think it is a tragedy; it is tremendously useful in analyzing and pinpointing problems in a piece of writing. No one really wants to spend his or her time diagramming, or learning how to diagram, a sentence (although I do know that one of my former graduate school professors, who claims to have somewhat masochistic tendencies, does diagram sentences in his free time—and freely admits it—to keep his writing and language analysis skills intact). However, this skill, once acquired, is invaluable. Once you know how to diagram sentences, you will be able to explain more effectively where an author's writing fails to meet the standard guidelines for good grammar and usage.

- Invest in one of the many excellent grammar review courses, books, or audiocassettes that are available (e.g., a good book to have on your reference shelf is *The Harbrace College Handbook,* and a good audiocassette is The Princeton Review *Grammar Smart* series). Believe me, if you can explain to your clients what a dangling or misplaced modifier is, for example—and the difference between the two—your clients (i.e., the ones who care about clarity) will consider you a grammatical god or goddess because so few people who are required to write as part of their daily jobs are aware of, or even recognize, the mistakes in their writing.

Hone your language skills by using these methods so that clients will want only you to edit their projects.

In addition to honing your language skills, you should consider brushing up on some other skills and abilities before setting out on your own as an editorial consultant. Skills in graphic design, layout, and type specification, for example, can be especially helpful. If you have a critical eye for the design and look of printed materials, or if you have design and layout experience, you can be of even more value to clients who need such expertise.

If you'll be working with publishers of books and journals, you will need an almost photographic memory to keep track of in-text discussions, as well as stylistic elements in each chapter and in front and back matter. Maintaining stylistic consistency throughout book-length manuscripts is important, so becoming acquainted with the various stylebooks that are available and memorizing their basic guidelines are essential to your success as a consultant.

Most publishers and corporate clients will specify which stylebook they follow. Each field (e.g., medicine, law, education, psychiatry, psychology, science, biology) has its own industry-standard stylebook that it follows almost religiously to maintain consistency across all publications. The stylebook, in essence, is that industry's bible. For instance, newspapers and magazines often use the *Associated Press Stylebook and Libel Manual*; book publishers, *The Chicago Manual of Style*; publishers of psychiatry and psychology topics, the *Publication Manual of the American Psychological Association*; publishers of health care and medical topics, *The American Medical Association Manual of Style: A Guide for Authors and Editors*; publishers of government information and issues, the *Government Printing Office Style Manual*; publishers of science and biology topics, *Scientific Style and Format: The Council of Biology Editors (CBE) Manual for Authors, Editors, and Publishers*; and law, *A Uniform System of Citation*.

With all the information available on the Internet (websites, e-zines, e-books), there's even some new stylebooks geared to editors in the electronic industry: *Electronic Styles: A Handbook for Citing Electronic Information, Second Edition,* and *The Columbia Guide to Online Style* (see Appendix B, "Books"). Both of these style manuals are worth investigating. In the years ahead, manuals for on-line style may become an essential addition to the editorial consultant's reference shelf as the citation of Internet sources becomes widespread in authors' works.

There are numerous dictionaries specific to each industry, which are also helpful when you are seeking industry-preferred spellings, capitalizations, abbreviations, and acronyms, along with their appropriate spell-outs. Most publishers that I have worked with rely on the current edition of *Webster's Collegiate Dictionary*. Keep an up-to-date edition on hand and consult it regularly. A searchable on-line version of *Merriam-Webster's Collegiate Dictionary* is available at <http://www.m-w.com>.

TIP!

When using Webster's, be certain to choose the first spelling or hyphenation whenever variations are listed because these are the preferred American spellings. Sometimes the British preferred spellings are listed secondarily—do not use these. You easily can identify these British spellings by double consonants (e.g., cancelled, labelled) or "s" in words such as *toward, backward, onward,* and *afterward*.

Clients even may compile and follow their own in-house style guidelines. They use these for all of their publications, as a supplement to the stylistic points enumerated in the industry-standard style manuals. If some of your clients do not have an in-house style guide, you can be the one to develop a stylebook for them so that their publications will be consistent from one issue, or printing, to the next.

Armed with current editions of *The Chicago Manual of Style* (which most book publishers prefer to use), *Webster's Collegiate Dictionary,* and a copy of your client's in-house style guide, you will have the foundation for building your copyediting reference shelf.

TIP!

Another essential and helpful aide to you and your clients when editing any project is the style sheet. The style sheet is simply a grid, labeled with letters *A* through *Z* and a heading for miscellaneous style matters. For all projects, whether a trifold brochure or multiauthor textbook, always make a style sheet to keep track of style points for text, including capitalization, spelling, numbers, units of measure, abbreviations, acronyms, and miscellaneous style choices used in tables, captions, figures, front matter, appendixes, and text cross-references. A style sheet is invaluable to you and your clients because it promotes consistency in all stylistic matters that emerge throughout the course of the entire text. The style sheet is also a helpful tool for those editors who are not blessed with a completely photographic memory.

When Is the Optimal Time to Leave My Full-Time Job?

You'll next need to consider the best time to leave your current full-time position. You cannot simply leave a full-time job and start your own business, no matter how great a dream that may seem. Unless you are independently wealthy—and let's face it, you're not if you are a full-time employee—you cannot walk into your boss' office, declare that you quit your job, and start up a business. Starting your business will be a slow, methodical process, and you will need to work hard to reach the day when you can tell your boss good-bye forever. No matter how giddy with excitement you may be about the prospect of leaving behind your job and boss, rein in that exhilaration until you are sufficiently prepared to leave.

Not only do you need the desire to start your own business and see it succeed, but you also need several clients. You will need at least three or more steady clients at the time of your business' start-up. You can probably get by with three clients, but several more would be advantageous in case at any time one, two, or all three of your clients cannot provide work assignments for you. This scenario does indeed happen from time to time, especially when clients' budgets are under review and get revised or when important contacts with whom you have developed a steady working relationship move into new positions within the company or leave the company altogether for career advancement.

TIP!

My best advice before starting your own business is to try to acquire freelance projects while you are still a full-time employee and work on them part-time, during the evenings or weekends. If you already have several freelance assignments to keep you busy when you leave your full-time position, the transition to your consultancy start-up will go more smoothly and your self-confidence in obtaining subsequent assignments will be established.

Have I Read Enough Background Material about Starting and Operating a Home-Based Business?

You wouldn't buy a new computer or car or start a new diet without reading as much background material as possible so that you could make educated decisions. Just as with making a costly purchase or changing your eating habits, you have many issues to consider and risks to face when starting your own business. Before you even take the initial steps in starting your business, you must do your homework. Hours of diligent research in advance will pay off in the long run in the form of a successful business that lasts for many years—and one that even may outlast you.

Read everything that you can about starting and operating your own business. Peruse the numerous how-to books that are available, as well as the many informative articles in magazines, newspapers, and trade publications. Good magazines to check out are *Entrepreneur's Home Office, Entrepreneur's Business Start-Ups, Home Business Magazine,* and *Independent Business,* periodicals with relevant articles for those working at home. Visit your local newsstand or bookstore and browse through the magazine rack to discover additional informative periodicals such as these.

TIP!

You can also surf the Internet for pertinent sites and information. If you are a member of America Online, for instance, there is a site dedicated to start-up businesses on the "Careers and Work" channel. A site such as this one, from an Internet provider, is an excellent place to begin your research because you can obtain lots of relevant background information in a minimum amount of time, all from one location. Yahoo.com and iVillage.com also have career and work channels replete with home and small business start-up information. Another excellent website is Nolo.com. There are also numerous home office–related e-zines, or electronic magazines, that you can read on-line for quick tips and advice targeted to small business owners and home-office workers. Several e-zines that may be of interest to you include *Small Business Computing, Home Office Computing, Home Worker, Work@Home Parents, Small Business Marketing News,* and *USA Home Business Journal.*

Delve into all of these resources and take copious notes in your business start-up journal so that you will be thoroughly prepared to start and run your own business. (See Suggested Readings for books on start-up and day-to-day operations of your business. See also Appendix B for helpful on-line resources.)

Have I Considered the Advantages and Disadvantages of a Home-Based Business?

After you've completed your initial research and background reading, sit down and thoroughly ponder the advantages and disadvantages of self-employment and a home-based business. There are quite a few pros and cons to consider, so you should spend some time seriously mulling over each one of them before you make the commitment to start and run your own business. You may want to record your thoughts and concerns in your business start-up journal as you read the following lists of advantages and disadvantages. Jotting down your thoughts may help clear the fog about some of the unknowns you'll confront as a newly self-employed individual.

Advantages

There are a number of wonderful advantages to being self-employed and running your own business, so think about the following pros:

- *Your time is your own.* You can now be as flexible as you like with your schedule because you'll be determining your work and personal time schedules. If you want to start your workday at 6 a.m. and work until 2 p.m., for example, you'll be done your workday early, leaving you time to tend to personal matters, such as picking up the children from school, food shopping, cleaning, or preparing dinner.

- *You'll have certain tax advantages by being self-employed and operating a home-based business.* There are many tax deductions that you will be eligible to take as part of the operating expenses for running a business from your home. As a full-time employee for someone else, you cannot take many of these tax deductions, such as costs involved in continuing your education or attending business-related seminars and conferences, joining professional organizations, subscribing to trade publications, or commuting to and from work, to name a few.

- *Clothing expenses will decrease.* You won't need to spend a fortune updating your business wardrobe because few people will see you wearing the same thing twice, especially if you'll have only a few meetings or limited contact with your clients. When you do need to meet with clients, you can get by with four or five business suits or dresses and a few casual separates, such as sweaters, skirts, and pants, that can be mixed and matched. Now that casual attire is more acceptable in many businesses, especially on Fridays or during the summer months, you might be able to get by with an entirely casual wardrobe. But try to keep or buy clothing constructed of fabrics that can be worn throughout several seasons, such as silk and lightweight wool blends, so that you'll get greater wear from them. Having a more simplified, interchangeable, seasonless wardrobe is a great advantage, particularly for women who tend to spend a lot of money accessorizing their business wardrobe with shoes, purses, jewelry, and pantyhose.

- *Automotive expenses will decrease.* You won't have a daily long-distance round-trip commute, so you should spend less on fuel and maintenance expenses. There should be less wear and tear on your vehicle, prolonging the life span of your car. If you work in a major city and pay monthly parking garage fees at your place of employment, those expenses will decline drastically as well.

- *You can create the kind of job that you like most.* You can take on the projects that you enjoy and that are most suitable to your expertise, and you can bypass those that are not particularly suitable to your skills. No one forces you to work on a particular assignment—and perhaps work on it with difficult people or with people whose personalities clash with yours.

- *There's no lost time due to weather-related incidents.* Whenever there's a snowstorm, ice storm, torrential rain, or even gale forces, you won't be wasting time cleaning off your car or sitting in traffic jams because of vehicular mishaps. Whether there's snow, sleet, rain, or hail, you'll simply walk to your home office and begin working.

- *Tedious interruptions will diminish, leaving you more time to focus on and complete your work.* No longer will you be delayed by the office gossip, who makes rounds to all the cubicles, regaling the latest office-related rumors. You won't have to take and handle irrelevant and unimportant telephone calls that eat up your workday. Likewise, you won't have to attend time-consuming, regularly scheduled status meetings that can throw off your entire workday—or even workweek.

- *You will not be limited to serve only local clientele.* With the widespread use of high-technology computers, modems, faxes, and e-mail, you really will be able to work with anyone, anywhere.

- *You will gain a tremendous sense of self-accomplishment and pride.* When you have completed an assignment and returned it to your client and that client immediately calls you back to check on your availability for the next project, your self-esteem will skyrocket. Or, if a client calls you back and asks if it would be all right to pass along your name and telephone number to a colleague who needs help with an editorial project, you will know that your work is of the highest quality and greatly respected. When your clients reassure you that your work is valued in these ways, you know that you have carved a niche for yourself and that you have created a need for your skills and expertise.

Disadvantages

Although you may feel exhilarated after considering the many advantages to self-employment, you must fully consider the following disadvantages as well:

- *At business start-up, your earnings probably will be less than those of your current full-time position.* When you start your business, there is a lot of downtime for which you are not paid. You will be spending time revising your resume; putting together a complete marketing package, including business cards, brochures, fliers, press releases, and other collateral materials; making telephone calls to solicit work or to contact established clients for work; and driving to and from the post office, office supply store, and library, as well as to your accountant's office from time to time. Remember, all of this time goes unpaid.

- *You are responsible for every aspect of your business.* As a self-employed business owner, you will perform numerous duties that you may not ever have been responsible for in the past. You will be responsible for bookkeeping, including tracking all of your income and expenses and preparing quarterly estimated taxes to be filed with your local tax division and the Internal Revenue Service; purchasing all of your office supplies and equipment; scheduling and organizing all of your work assignments; soliciting new clients and keeping in contact with established clients; maintaining a steady work flow; preparing marketing and advertising materials; preparing a business plan; handling any paperwork for special applications, licensing, and professional memberships; preparing all client proposals, contracts, and invoices; and seeking and finding your own health care benefits plan (if you need one), tax advisor, legal advisor, and business banking services. No one else will handle these duties for you.

- *If you don't work, you don't get paid.* Keep in mind that when you are self-employed, you no longer enjoy the benefits of paid sick leave, vacation or personal days, holidays, and maternity leave. Any days that you take off or any time spent away from your business goes unpaid.

- *There are no steady, reliable paychecks as there are in full-time employment.* When you do receive payment from your clients, always remember that about one-third of your income will go toward payment of county, state, and federal taxes. So, be warned: do not spend all of your money before you have earned it. You also should keep in mind that some of your clients will pay your invoices in a timelier manner than will others. Some accounting offices have rapid turnaround times, so you may receive payment on your invoice within two to four weeks. Other clients may have an out-of-state home office where contractor invoices are sent, so you may not see a check for 90 days or even longer. Still other clients may completely lag in paying you or have a lapse in memory after you've sent an invoice, and you will need to send out a payment overdue notice every 30 days as a reminder. This last scenario happens infrequently with large corporations, and even small businesses, because invoices are submitted to and processed by an accounting department, which must uphold certain legal guidelines in paying vendors and contractors. However, nonpayment of an invoice is a situation that may develop when working one-on-one with an individual rather than a company (see Case Example 3, which follows this bulleted list). Whether that individual is a friend, friend of a friend, relative, or colleague of one of your clients, do not be intimidated. Always request payment for services rendered and follow up with reminders, in writing, with a telephone call or e-mail or fax, or in person, as often as necessary. Nonpayment of invoices leads to bad feelings between you and your clients and may even lead to time-consuming legal proceedings, which you definitely want to avoid.

- *Being a self-employed editorial consultant often can be lonely.* Office camaraderie no longer exists when you are self-employed, so if you enjoy working surrounded by lots of people, being alone so often and working in complete silence can be a major psychological adjustment. There are no co-workers nearby to confer or discuss ideas with when you have tough decisions to make, and there is no second set of eyes to proofread your work before it is returned to the client. Managers or higher-ups won't be looking over your shoulder to see that you are completing your work, and they won't be handing you your next assignment. You, alone, are responsible for keeping work steadily flowing in and out of your home office. You must be motivated enough to rise each day and begin working on—or soliciting—editorial assignments.

- *If you do a good job, there is no guarantee that a client will call you with more editorial assignments.* On the other hand, if you do a poor job, you can be certain that your client will not call you for assistance again, unless that client desperately needs help. However, even if you do an excellent job for a client, you cannot be assured that you'll receive steady work from that client. Budgets and in-house staff are always subject to change, and those changes may impact you as an independent contractor. Never sit on your laurels when you have completed a project. Always seek and schedule your next assignment *before* you have completed the one on which you are currently working.

- *There is no staff to call on when you have technical problems with your office equipment or need office supplies.* If something suddenly goes wrong with your computer or printer, or if you run out of paper and diskettes and your client's deadline is tomorrow, you cannot simply reach for the telephone, dial an extension, and soon receive technical assistance or supplies. There is no in-house computer expert to fix your computer glitches or purchasing department to handle your requests. You must always be prepared for the unexpected. Try to establish reliable contacts who can provide technical assistance if you have problems with office equipment that you cannot figure out on your own, and try to keep your office supplies well-stocked to avoid last-minute deficits when you most need supplies.

- *You may have difficulty separating your home and your work life.* Because your office will be part of your home, problems may arise that you did not have while working in an office away from home. If your home office has a door, close it at the end of each day so that you will not be overwhelmed with guilt or anxiety every time you walk by your office and see unfinished projects on your desk. Also, get a telephone answering machine and use it *always* to screen all calls. Family members, friends, and telemarketers will interrupt you throughout the day. Since you are at home, they tend to believe that you are not really working and it's all right to call as often as they like—or even barge into your office. Be firm with everyone who tries to lure you away from your work and fast-approaching deadlines with tempting offers of shopping, lunch, or happy hour. Establish your workday schedule, set limits, and let them know about those limits in advance; for example, you will only take personal calls before 8:30 a.m. or after 4:30 p.m., or you will meet them for only a one-hour lunch.

- *The euphemism "feast or famine" holds true when you have your own business.* You will develop a clear sense of the ebb and flow of your workload after you have been self-employed for two to three years or longer. There will be times when you must work late into the night, through the weekends, or through holidays and special occasions just so you can meet your clients' deadlines. At other times, your days will be spent cleaning out your files, deleting old files from your computer's hard drive, organizing or rearranging your office, or preparing your quarterly tax figures for your accountant. On these "off" days, remember that you won't be getting paid. Therefore, save your income systematically until you can gauge your workload and payment schedules.

Case Example 3

I had agreed to assist an aspiring author, a colleague of one of my clients, who had written several children's stories that he wanted critiqued and edited. I reviewed, critiqued, and edited each story thoroughly, completing the job in approximately two weeks. I additionally provided the author a list of potential children's book publishers to which he could submit his manuscripts, along with copies of several pertinent articles detailing current trends in the children's book market and how to prepare a cover letter and proposal that would win editors' attention.

Although I gave the author these extras and rapidly completed the assignment, I did not receive payment until nearly a year had elapsed—and only after I had sent several payment overdue notices and periodically left voice mails with gentle reminders that I had not yet received payment on my invoice.

TIP!

A major caveat to the editorial consultant: never expect immediate payment for services rendered. For clients who procrastinate or are consistently late with invoice payments, always send periodic payment-overdue reminders, at least every 30 days. Be persistent and you eventually will receive payment for your services.

Have I Saved Enough Money for Start-Up?

After pondering all the pros and cons of being self-employed and running your own business, the final—but perhaps most crucial—consideration is your current financial status.

If you are the single source of income for your household, you will need to save about a year's salary and expenses in advance of your business' start-up. When I started my business, more than 10 years ago, most sources recommended saving about six months' salary and expenses. To be financially safe, I would recommend saving for a full year, especially if yours is the sole income of the household. If you are married and your spouse has a steady source of income, as well as a health benefits plan that covers you as a dependent, you can probably get by with six months' savings. However, again, saving one year's worth of your salary and expenses is optimal, especially if you are currently employed and your secondary income is greatly depended on to meet all of your household expenses.

If you do not have health care coverage on a spouse's benefits plan, you will need to buy your own plan when you start your business. Costs for individual health care coverage, as opposed to group coverage, can be quite high; be certain to shop around for the best premium. As a self-employed individual, you'll be allowed to deduct a certain percentage of your health care insurance premium on your tax return, but be sure to consult your tax advisor. In the future, if tax laws change, there's hope that self-employed individuals may be able to deduct 100% of their health plan costs. Currently, however, a full deduction is not allowed.

Chapter 2

Step 2: Take a How-To Course or Seminar and Seek Free Advice

Once you have taken the crucial first step—that is, you have considered the many practicalities as well as advantages and disadvantages of starting and running your own editorial consulting business—you should investigate how-to courses or seminars. Brief, noncredit courses and seminars will provide helpful background information that assists you in your efforts to get your business up and running. If you are serious about making the commitment to start and run an editorial consulting business, and are mentally and financially prepared to persevere through good times and bad, how-to courses can provide you with beneficial introductory details. Such courses can enlighten you about the day-to-day tasks and responsibilities involved in running your own business so that you won't be completely uninformed, or misinformed, at start-up. Your local offices of the U.S. Small Business Administration (SBA), U.S. Chamber of Commerce, or Home-Based Business Association are all good places to start, as are community colleges. Call and request a schedule of seminars, workshops, and continuing education courses, and inquire about their fees.

In addition to exploring courses and training in home-based business start-up, networking with other editorial consultants or freelancers and seeking their advice on maintaining a home-based business is a good way to introduce you to the realities of self-employment. Talking with someone who does—or has done—the type of editorial work you would like to do can be invaluable in your decision-making process. A big advantage to this source of information is that the advice comes absolutely free of charge.

Small Business Administration

One of the best sources for introductory information, seminars, and workshops on how to start and operate a business is the SBA. This federal agency provides informative guidance and training to small-business owners throughout the United States. SBA training and conferences take place in each state, and some courses are even available on-line. Your local SBA office may have its own library as well. Here, you'll find helpful literature at your disposal as you take the initial steps in business start-up.

SBA workshops are available for reasonable fees that won't cause financial setbacks in your start-up budget. For example, in my state, for less than $100, you can take a 2-day workshop covering business start-up topics such as entrepreneurship, management, legal issues, preparing a business plan, marketing and advertising, finances, recordkeeping, and preparing your taxes. The SBA holds these introductory workshops and courses throughout the year, statewide. Check the blue pages of your local telephone directory for a listing of your state's SBA office, and call for further information on seminars offered in your area. Or you may want to check the SBA's website for a detailed calendar of events in your state at <http://www.sbaonline.sba.gov>.

A service offshoot of the SBA is the Service Corps of Retired Executives (SCORE). This group is also listed in the blue pages of your telephone directory. SCORE provides outreach, mentoring, and counseling to start-up business owners. If you call SCORE, a representative can match you to a former local business executive who has experience in your field of interest. You will receive free counseling and advice for starting and building your business.

In my state, SCORE has sponsored free one-on-one counseling sessions at branches of the county library. A SCORE representative is available on the designated date and time at the library, so you can meet with someone in person and discuss your business ideas and plans. Take advantage of these counseling and mentoring services, if they are available where you live, because useful information and advice are provided to you at no cost.

Chamber of Commerce

Your local Chamber of Commerce can be another important source of start-up information. Visit the U.S. Chamber of Commerce website, <http://www.uschamber.org>, or check the blue pages of your local telephone directory to locate the Chamber of Commerce office nearest to you.

The Chamber of Commerce exists to address a wide variety of business concerns. It offers introductory courses for new business owners, and representatives are available to provide practical advice on starting and running your business, as well as assistance with developing your business plan.

If you visit this agency's website, also check out <http://www.chamberbiz.com>. Here you'll discover useful checklists and tools at your fingertips that will aid in getting your business up and running in no time. There are checklists for business start-up considerations, cash needs statements, and examples of business and marketing plan components. You can peruse your local Chamber of Commerce's calendar of events for details about the group's upcoming meetings. You may want to attend a few of these meetings to network with business owners in your area. Chamber meetings also might provide you the opportunity to locate additional contacts in the editorial or publishing field.

National Association of Home-Based Businesses

Another organization well worth checking out is the National Association of Home-Based Businesses (NAHBB). The purpose of this association is to help its members successfully develop their home-based businesses and unify them as a group. Check the associations listed in your yellow pages telephone directory to determine if such an affiliate association exists in your area. You may want to look at the NAHBB's website at <http://usahomebusiness.com>, which has additional links to helpful websites and resources for home-based business owners.

In my state, the Home-Based Business Association (HBBA) holds monthly breakfast meetings, lasting about an hour or so. For a minimal fee, you can attend the meeting, check out the organization, and acquire timely, relevant information on home-based business matters, such as planning, marketing and publicity, setting up a home office, tax planning and preparation, legal issues, and more. Meetings, featuring guest speakers, are a forum for the exchange of ideas between entrepreneurs and established business owners and for the discussion of issues affecting owners of small home-based businesses. Networking opportunities also exist, for the purposes of generating and expanding business leads and contacts.

If you become a member of your local HBBA, you may enjoy the benefit of a free monthly consultation with a seasoned HBBA member whose expertise you can consult. Don't be timid about seeking such help and advice. Take advantage of these types of opportunities, because they are designed to expand your networking resources and aid in business development.

Another inexpensive way to obtain preliminary home-based business information is to attend an HBBA-sponsored trade show. Each year, the HBBA in my locale holds an expo. For about $10 a ticket, you can tour exhibits and displays of other home-based business owners and attend seminars covering topics such as financing and loans, accounting, computer technology, marketing, and insurance. You may even get additional inspiration and ideas for ways to market your professional services.

Community Colleges

Another good source for brief, low-cost courses or seminars on starting your business is your local community college. Contact the continuing education offices of some of the community colleges in your area to obtain a course catalog and discover what courses or seminars are available. Many community colleges offer introductory noncredit courses that can be completed in one day, or a few days—at most—for a nominal fee. For a limited investment of time and money, you'll receive additional valuable information that can help as you launch your business.

Consultants and Freelancers

Excellent advice, at no cost to you, is available when you network with everyone you know until you acquire the names and telephone numbers of consultants, freelancers, or independent contractors who run or have run an editorial services–related business. Contact each one and speak with him or her to discover the realities of being self-employed and running a home-based business.

If you have exhausted your network of family, friends, and business colleagues and still come up with no names and telephone numbers, try contacting one of the professional organizations discussed in Chapter 3 and request a membership directory. These directories list the names, telephone numbers, and specialties of members—some of whom may live in your area. You might be able to speak with an editorial expert who does the type of work you would enjoy doing most. If you are not a member of the organization, however, the representative who handles your call may not be willing to send you a copy of the directory. Be prepared to have your request denied or to pay a fee to obtain the directory.

Another option for acquiring names and telephone numbers of other consultants in your area is to call and speak with the communications or public relations directors of businesses in your community. Tell the director that you are researching opportunities for editorial consultants or independent contractors, and then inquire whether he or she ever uses contractual editorial services. If the response is yes, ask the director if he or she could refer you to one or two of the editorial consultants for that business so that you may conduct an informational interview with them. In most instances, the communications or public relations director will oblige and provide the name and telephone number of at least one consultant who would be willing to talk with you.

As mentioned previously, by attending the meetings of your local Chamber of Commerce or HBBA, you can network with and perhaps acquire the names of editorial professionals whom you could interview.

TIP!

When you contact the consultants themselves, they are usually more than happy to hold an informational interview with you. The only touchy topic that they may want to avoid is income. Most consultants and independent contractors will not be forthcoming about their rates or fees because they want to remain competitive in the field. Out of courtesy and respect for the interviewees, do not monopolize their time, and be certain to avoid questions related to rates and annual income. A follow-up note of thanks is also appropriate for anyone who takes the time to offer information and advice, so be certain to get the correct spelling of the interviewee's name and his or her complete address. That interviewee could be an important business contact in the years ahead, so be thoughtful and polite.

Chapter 3

Step 3: Contact Professional Organizations

*P*rofessional organizations can be of great assistance to the editorial consultant who has begun his or her own venture. By contacting several professional organizations, requesting their literature, or checking out their websites on the Internet, you can evaluate which organizations may be of most help to you, depending on the type of editorial work you like to do.

As mentioned in Chapter 2, you can obtain a wealth of helpful preliminary details regarding business start-up by contacting your local offices of the Small Business Administration, Chamber of Commerce, and Home-Based Business Association. Much of the information that you'll receive from these groups will be low cost, if not free, just for checking out the group's services to small, home-based business owners.

To locate other professional groups that may be of interest and help to you as an editorial consultant (e.g., the Council of Science Editors, Editorial Freelancers Association [EFA], International Association of Business Communicators, Association for Women in Communications), start by checking the Internet for websites or by paging through the *Literary Market Place* (see Appendix B, "Books"), *Writer's Essential Desk Reference* (see Suggested Readings), and other directories targeted to writers and editors for their listings. These directories provide the association's current addresses, telephone numbers, and in some cases, websites. Organizations that are reputable and longstanding are included.

A partial listing of helpful groups also is included in this book, in Appendix B, "Professional Organizations."

Benefits to Joining an Organization

Joining a professional organization is beneficial to your business because these groups provide a wide variety of informative and professional services for their members. Most publish a newsletter and membership directory, some of which are distributed regionally, or even nationally, to leaders in the business community. Membership directories can be a valuable marketing tool when you are just starting your business. I've received several work assignments from business leaders who paged through a membership directory and located my name, telephone number, and services that I provide. By including your name, business' name, address, telephone numbers, e-mail address, and editorial specialties (e.g., medical textbook copyediting, developmental fiction editing, newsletter editing), you'll reach important business contacts or other members who may need your assistance and expertise.

In addition to newsletters and membership directories, some organizations publish listings of full-time, part-time, and contractual editorial jobs, as well as internships. Some groups have job hotlines that only their members may access for leads on temporary, full-time, or part-time assignments, either on-site or on a freelance basis. You'll probably pay an additional fee to use the group's job hotline, but it is worth the extra fee for two important reasons: 1) a job hotline can greatly reduce the amount of time you'll spend researching and soliciting clients when you are just establishing your business, and 2) as your business grows, you can use the hotlines as a resource for quick-turnaround assignments when you are between jobs for your established clients. Some associations, such as the EFA, now offer their job hotline information on-line.

As a member of a professional organization serving editorial or communications consultants, you'll be invited to attend seminars, workshops, and continuing education courses, at a discounted rate. Take advantage of these events to improve and hone your editorial skills. You also might consider attending the organization's annual conference or being an exhibitor at an industry-related trade show, which are both good environments for networking and expanding your client contacts. Some national organizations (e.g., the EFA) have local or regional chapters that meet regularly, perhaps nearby where you live, to discuss current issues and topics related to your specialty, such as medical writing and editing, scholarly books editing, fiction editing, and business communications editing, to name a few. These meetings also offer great opportunities for networking, as well as brainstorming editorial issues that arise during the course of your various projects.

Other benefits of becoming a member of a professional organization include the following:

- Arbitration services to recoup payments from nonpaying or late-paying clients

- Discounted health insurance plans

- Legal services

- Internet listservs for contacting other members for editorial guidance, advice, and discussions

TIP!

Assess multiple professional organizations when you are just beginning your editorial consulting business. Then, join two or three groups that most interest you. This step can be costly, since most professional organizations charge membership dues of $100 or more per year. However, in my opinion, it is necessary to join more than one group, for a year or longer, so that you can determine most effectively which one provides you with the most valuable, accessible services for your money.

Once you have been a practicing editorial consultant for several years and have discovered your niche, you may want to join one of the specialized professional organizations listed in Appendix B. I have only scratched the surface with the groups listed there. I am certain that you will discover many more organizations as you conduct your research, but always remember to investigate each thoroughly and join only those that are reputable and well established.

Questions to Ask When Evaluating an Organization

As you contact the professional organizations that interest you, ask questions that will help you in the evaluation process. Keep track of each organization's responses in your business start-up journal so that you may easily refer to them, for instance, when comparing each group's benefits and services.

Answers to the following eight pertinent questions will help you size up the groups that are most suitable for you:

1. When was your organization established?

2. Do you have a local/regional chapter serving my area?

3. What are your annual membership dues?

4. Is there a discount for dues paid in advance (e.g., $100 if paying for the year or $180 if paying for two years)?

5. What services do you offer to members?

6. What publications do members receive?

7. What industry-related events do you sponsor (e.g., trade shows, expos, conferences, workshops, seminars, educational courses)?

8. Do you conduct periodic membership surveys to obtain feedback about members' needs and wants?

TIP!

The preceding questions hinge on three important considerations: 1) locality, 2) dues, and 3) services. The second question is a significant criterion in evaluating a professional organization because you want to be afforded full advantage of the group's services, regardless of where you live. For example, I recently discontinued membership in one association because all events and job information were targeted to members centrally located to the association's business offices. Although this group, at one time, talked of forming a subchapter serving members living in my area, the subgroup never evolved while I was a member. Professional organizations at times can seem cliquish, catering to the needs of only a select few who are lucky enough to be residing in the same area where the organization is based. If you believe that a professional group to which you belong neglects a certain portion of its paying members, you may want to reevaluate your membership status. Or, you may want to recommend that a subchapter be formed to serve members in your locality, and then see to it that the subchapter materializes if promised. After all, you don't want to waste business funds on membership dues where you receive limited benefits and services for the dollars invested.

Caveats to Joining an Organization

After you have contacted the organizations that interest you, and narrowed your choices, it's time to join. There are two important caveats to remember about joining professional organizations:

1. *Do not become a compulsive joiner.* Be selective about the organizations with which you want to affiliate your editorial consulting business. As mentioned previously, when you are evaluating organizations, join two or three that are the most reputable, well established, and valuable to your career. Then, after you have been a member for some time and have had the chance to determine which group or groups offer the most relevant benefits and services, narrow your membership to the top one or two.

2. *Do not become a professional organization "groupie."* Especially when you are starting your business, do not waste precious time by attending the many nonessential breakfast, lunch, and dinner meetings or other social gatherings these groups hold over the course of a year. There certainly is nothing wrong in attending a few meetings, especially when they feature guest speakers discussing pertinent issues related to your business. However, you may become so dependent on attending these group functions and chatting with your peers that nothing gets accomplished toward maintaining your business and seeing it grow and succeed. Don't ignore business obligations and sacrifice valuable work time to socialize. You need to achieve a healthy balance between time spent

working and socializing. Be selective with your attendance of the organization's meetings or other functions, and show up for the ones that will benefit you and your growing business.

Chapter 4

Step 4: Find a Qualified Certified Public Accountant

$\mathcal{B}$efore you even begin doing business as a consultant, it is essential that you seek and find a qualified certified public accountant (CPA). Although your best friend's Uncle Mort may prepare taxes for all of his family members and friends, do not rely on him to handle your small-business taxes. Numerous tax laws regarding small businesses change yearly, and a CPA must keep informed of all these changes. If you don't know a CPA, you can contact your state's association of certified public accountants for a referral, or try your local chapter of the Small Business Administration (SBA). The SBA conducts introductory workshops on business start-up, including tax preparation. The instructor of an SBA-sponsored business start-up workshop, or similar seminars or educational courses offered by other organizations, may be able to provide you with leads on CPA services. Even the bank where you plan to open your small-business accounts can be a good source for obtaining a CPA referral.

You will need the services and expert advice of a CPA for a number of business-related matters, including the following:

- Determining how you should set up your business (i.e., sole proprietorship, partnership, corporation)

- Assisting with financial planning for your business checking and/or savings account

- Advising you regarding business expenses and income

- Advising you regarding estimated quarterly tax payments

- Handling and filing year-end federal, state, and county tax forms

- Handling other tax-related paperwork and correspondence required by the federal and local taxing authorities

- Handling any tax audits should they arise

Setting Up Your Business

Your CPA will help you determine how you first should set up your business, and there are three options to consider:

1. Sole proprietorship

2. Partnership

3. Corporation

There are distinct tax advantages and disadvantages to each option, but your tax advisor will give you expert guidance when the time comes. When I began my editorial services business, for example, I started out as a sole proprietorship, and after seven years in business, I incorporated as Frutchey Publishing

Services, Inc., because I wanted to expand my business in the years ahead and possibly add employees. A sole proprietorship served me well at business start-up, when I conducted business under my name, and incorporation later helped me establish a competitive edge as I discovered my niche and expanded my services and clientele. Rather than simply using your own name under which to conduct business, incorporation lends an air of professionalism to your consultancy, even if you are a one-woman, or -man, show.

TIP!

If you choose to incorporate your business, do not let your tax advisor or anyone else pressure you into seeking legal counsel to file incorporation papers. You can complete the process yourself, which is simply a matter of filling out the required paperwork and articles of incorporation from your state's department of assessment and taxation. If you complete the paperwork yourself, you'll pay about $50 rather than up to $500, the customary charges if you enlist the services of a lawyer. The procedure is simple and takes less than an hour. Do it yourself, and you'll save almost ten times the amount in lawyer's fees.

Opening Bank Accounts for Your Business

Once you have located a reliable CPA to help guide your business' start-up and maintenance, he or she may suggest that you open separate business checking and savings accounts in your name (i.e., your name is on the account, but you are "doing business as" the name you have created for your company) or your business' name, and that you obtain a tax identification number (TIN) rather than using your social security number.

As a protective measure, it is always best to separate your business finances from your personal finances. Unfortunately, we live in a litigious society, and people sue each other every day over the most minor concerns, so protect yourself and your personal finances from any litigation that may develop over the years.

In addition, you may want to consult your CPA for a recommendation on banks that specialize in small-business services. He or she may be able to direct you to a bank in your area that provides checking and savings accounts with low or no monthly maintenance fees, free checks, credit cards, automated teller machine (ATM) cards, and low-interest-rate small-business loans—all important considerations when establishing your business banking relationship.

Tracking Business Expenses and Income

Your tax advisor will also guide you in keeping accurate account of all business-related expenses and income. Make it a habit to keep all receipts and to record all expenses and income at the end of each month. You may want to record all expenses and income at the end of each quarter, especially if you are too pressed for time to handle monthly tracking. But remember: haphazard recordkeeping only hurts you and your business in the long run. Find the most suitable schedule for you and stick with it.

In some instances, you will not be issued receipts for a business expense, such as when you need to use parking meters and copy machines. Therefore, in those situations, you should keep plenty of rolls of quarters handy so that you can document the date, client's name, project, and purpose of the expense on the coin wrappers. Believe it or not, these paper wrappers qualify as a receipt. Rather than omitting these expenses altogether because you have no receipt for services rendered, you can keep the wrappers to record all of them—and they're documented on paper.

To keep track of your business expenses and income, a simple bookkeeping program, such as *Quicken*, will help you remain organized throughout the year, whether you update your records monthly or quarterly. At the end of each quarter, you can generate a report of your expenses and income, which you then can forward to your CPA. These reports can help your CPA determine quarterly estimated tax payments owed to the Internal Revenue Service (IRS) and local tax authorities.

As your business grows, you may want to enlist the services of a bookkeeper. When your business has grown to the point of needing such assistance and you can relinquish bookkeeping responsibilities to someone else, you will then have even more time to focus on day-to-day business operations.

Making Quarterly Estimated Tax Payments

As a self-employed consultant, you'll pay your business taxes quarterly, in January, April, June, and September. It may take some getting used to, especially if you've prepared your taxes only once a year as a full-time employee. But as you pay your estimated taxes quarterly, it becomes habit.

There are two key things to remember about paying quarterly estimated taxes:

1. *Do not wait until the end of the tax year to sort through your paystubs and expense receipts.* If you are really busy with your daily work, you will be tempted to put off your bookkeeping duties until a more appropriate time—such as at the end of the year, when the tax deadline looms. I have learned through trial and error that waiting is not an acceptable method because it is not conducive to smooth, efficient operations. After an entire year has elapsed, you will not be able to re-create your expenses from the first quarter, let alone recall what expenses correspond with which client's project. You may not enjoy working with numbers, but do not procrastinate with this task. It's better to systematically track and enter your income and expenses weekly, monthly, or quarterly, to avoid year-end headaches and hair pulling.

2. *Do not send your tax payments late and never underpay your estimated quarterly taxes.* As you track your expenses and income, your CPA can advise you about what your quarterly tax payment should be. After you've paid quarterly taxes for some time, and it becomes familiar, you won't shortchange the IRS, local tax authorities, or yourself. Pencil in the due dates for your taxes each quarter in your daytimer to avoid late payments. You do not want to send up any red flags to the IRS or state department of taxation by sending in your payments late, underpaying, or omitting payments altogether. Always keep in mind that underpayment or nonpayment of your quarterly taxes can lead to a big fat required payment at the end of the tax year, perhaps when funds are running low and you can least afford it. Engage in any of these red-flag activities, and you could be facing an audit—another headache you don't need.

Case Example

One year, my ex-CPA simply forgot about the "tax advising" portion of his duties, to my great detriment. He did not guide me about quarterly payments, and so I waited until the end of the year to pay. I ended up owing the state and federal government more than $3,000—soon after having given birth to my daughter. Because of his lack of advice, and my neglect in sending in regular estimated quarterly tax payments on my income that year, my family suffered a financial crunch at a time when we least needed that hassle.

Although at first you may find it difficult and overwhelming to keep track of multiple editorial and tax deadlines, always be aware of your income, expenses, and due dates for tax payments. Stay organized, write everything down, and make your payments on time to avoid tax-related problems. In addition, always consult your CPA for guidance whenever you have a question or whenever something seems not quite right. And again, be certain to check into his or her tax-advising credentials in advance so that you won't be misinformed or misled.

Handling Tax-Related Paperwork and Other Matters

A dependable—and professional—CPA additionally will relieve you of the stress and burden of tax-related paperwork and correspondence required from time to time by the federal, state, and county taxing authorities. For instance, if the IRS has no record of, or accidentally omits, one of your quarterly payments, your CPA can handle the necessary correspondence documenting your payments. Or, if you incorporate your business and your state taxing authority requires you to file an annual statement of personal property for your business, your CPA likewise can handle the appropriate paperwork.

If your business is ever audited, you definitely will need to notify and consult your CPA for his or her assistance and expertise. Audits can be prevented if your are following the guidance of a reliable and professional CPA who keeps apprised of the ever-changing tax laws and regulations. According to the IRS' website, about 2% of small business and about 1% of individual tax returns are audited each year. The Nolo.com website points out that although the chances of your being audited are small in any one given year, over the long run of your tax-paying lifetime as a self-employed individual you stand a 50% chance of being audited. The IRS scrutinizes the returns of self-employed individuals who have home-based businesses because, according to Nolo.com, "the IRS believes they cheat more often than wage earners." Most audits result from a combination of poor recordkeeping habits and blatant disregard for tax-reporting laws and guidelines. Finding a qualified CPA in whom you can place your trust whenever tax-related questions and issues arise can help you avoid an audit. Helpful websites for your concerns about audits are <http://www.irs.ustreas.gov>, <http://www.nolo.com>, and <http://www.wwwebtax.com>. The Webtax.com site also has links to the American Institute of Certified Public Accountants, the IRS, and other government tax links, all of which you may find helpful.

If you are audited, the IRS will want to examine your finances and investigate important issues such as, among others, failing to report significant business income, writing off personal living expenses (i.e., autos, entertainment, meals, vacations, furnishings, clothing) as business expenses, and maintaining an extravagant lifestyle that does not correspond with a low reported income (i.e., expensive cars, clothing, jewelry, homes, and home furnishings).

The IRS is able to obtain your financial records, so if you deposit unreported income into your personal or business accounts, the IRS may know of your practices. If anything looks awry on your tax return, beware. The IRS may target you for an audit.

Chapter 5

Step 5: Consider the Practicalities of Running Your Home Office

Critical to the success of your editorial consulting business is careful consideration of the everyday, practical matters that inevitably arise. Not only do you need a business plan to keep you on course for the long-term, but you also need an action plan for short-term challenges that require your immediate attention. By carefully considering and planning for the following important matters in advance of your business' start-up, you'll save yourself a multitude of time and worry in the days ahead. You may want to record your initial responses to the following questions in your business start-up journal, as well as your detailed plans for handling the everyday business-related issues discussed in each section of this chapter.

- How do I determine a fee schedule that's competitive but fair to my clients and myself?

- Where should I set up my work space?

- What office furniture, equipment, and supplies do I need?

- How should I finance my start-up expenses?

- Do I have resources and a plan to overcome unexpected disasters such as computer equipment failure?

- How do I best handle nonpaying clients, rush assignments, and conflicting client obligations?

- How can I prevent work-related stress and burnout?

Setting Your Fees

Fees are an important issue to consider because as an independent contractor, your livelihood depends on your ability to earn a competitive income. As an editorial consultant, you can expect to earn a wide range of fees, depending on the type of service you provide, the size of your clients' businesses, and the clients' budgets for editorial assignments.

There are several excellent sources available to help guide you in establishing fees for various services, including the following:

- *Writer's Market*—Each year, Writer's Digest Books publishes this quintessential writers' resource, listing the editorial needs and submissions guidelines of thousands of publishers. This book also includes a detailed section, "How Much Should I Charge," which lists the range of fees you can expect for various writing and editorial services provided to various industries such as advertising; public relations; audiovisual and electronic communications; book publishing; business, computer, scientific, and technical; and educational and literary. The *Writer's Market* is a good place to start, just to get a clearer idea of the fees you might charge your clients.

- *Editorial Freelancers Association Rates and Business Practices Survey*—The Editorial Freelancers Association (EFA), a professional organization for independent and freelance editors, last surveyed its members in 1996 and published a detailed account of responses to questions regarding business practices and rates. The survey reports typical rates charged for 10 editorial services, including abstracting, copyediting, indexing, photo editing, proofreading, research, and writing. Rates are listed in dollars per hour earned in three industries: 1) publishing, 2) corporate, and 3) nonprofit. If you join the EFA or any one of the many professional organizations available to editors and/or writers, inquire about receiving a copy of its current rates and practices guidelines. Surveys such as the one published by the EFA are invaluable in helping you determine your fees and remain competitive as an independent editor.

- *National Writers Union Guide to Freelance Rates and Standard Practice*—The National Writers Union (NWU) comprises approximately 4,000 members, most of whom are freelance writers. Included in the NWU's book, however, is a chapter on corporate and nonprofit rates and communications practices, which is relevant to editors as well. This book is worth taking a look at for even more background information on industry rates and practices (see Suggested Readings).

- *Other editorial consultants or freelance editors*—If you know someone who currently works as an independent editor, ask him or her directly about fees for services. There is one caveat in taking this approach: most consultants or freelancers do not like to reveal what their clients pay. In an effort to remain competitive, and also because each editorial assignment is so different, your source may not want to give you a straight answer about what you can charge or earn for your services.

From my experience as an editorial consultant, I can confirm that payments for editorial assignments vary greatly, based upon the level of technicality of the materials you are editing as well as upon your clients' line of business—and especially their budgets.

On the East Coast (e.g., in the Baltimore-Washington metropolitan area, where I conduct business), you can expect to earn—on average—between $15 per hour and $75 per hour. Again, keep in mind that these figures depend upon the type of service you provide and type of client with whom you are working. For example, you might be paid $15 to $20 per hour for proofreading services that you provide to a nonprofit organization that hires you to review its newsletter or collateral marketing materials, whereas a larger corporate entity might pay you $25 to $30 hourly for the same service, for the same types of publications. For special assignment writing or developmental editing, a small company might pay $25 per hour, but a corporate conglomerate may double or even triple that amount.

However, don't fall into the trap of rationalizing that because larger corporations have the bigger budgets you should only focus on approaching them as potential clients. Although you may earn a lower hourly rate for services provided to a small or nonprofit firm, your workload might be greater and more consistent from such a company. Smaller companies need the assistance of independent contractors more frequently. Because many small companies and nonprofit groups usually cannot afford to hire full-time staff to complete their editorial work, they often rely on the ongoing assistance of independent contractors. With larger businesses and corporate conglomerates, you may have the opportunity to assist them on an as-needed basis only (e.g., annually or semiannually), because these types of businesses usually have the full-time staff to cover their editorial workloads.

Determining Your Hourly Rate

As discussed previously, there are a number of methods you can use to determine a competitive hourly rate:

- You can consult one of the many references and resources available to editors and writers (see Suggested Readings and Appendix B, "Books").

- You can use a professional association's membership survey.

- You can conduct a market survey of your own in the area where you live and will be establishing your business.

One of the best formulas that I have found helpful in determining a competitive hourly rate for editorial services appears in the *1999 Writer's Market*. Based on the guidelines provided there, you can establish a baseline hourly fee; add an appropriate percentage for expenses, overhead, and profit; and then calculate your minimum hourly rate for any job you accept.

The following example for determining an hourly fee is adapted from the *1999 Writer's Market*:

1. Start with a reasonable annual salary that you'd like to earn, say $38,000.

2. Divide that number by the estimated number of hours you'll work during the year, say 32 hours per week or 1,664 hours per year. Be conservative to start because you will not be working a full 40-hour week right away. Keep in mind that some time is devoted to administrative tasks tending to your own business, which is not billable time for your clients.

3. Your baseline figure is therefore $38,000 ÷ 1,664 or 22.84, which I would round up to $23 per hour.

4. Add 33% to your baseline ($7.59) for expenses your full-time employer used to cover or deduct (e.g., health insurance, taxes, retirement funds, social security).

5. Add a 10% profit margin ($2.30).

6. Add your overhead expenses. You can calculate these by tallying all expenses for one year and then dividing by the number of hours you actually worked during the year. If your expenses totaled $3,000, for example, and you worked 1,664 hours, your overhead costs are $1.80 per hour.

7. Add the above figures to determine the minimum hourly rate you should charge a client for each job: $23 + $7.59 + $2.30 + $1.80 = $34.69 or $35 *per hour.*

TIP!

Some companies will tell you what they can afford to pay you for your services, based on their budgets for certain projects. Others will ask you to quote either an hourly or per-project figure. In the latter situation, I have found that it is better to quote an hourly rate for clients rather than quoting a lump-sum-per-project figure because you never can gauge exactly the amount of work a project entails until you begin working on it. This point particularly holds true in the book publishing industry. Invariably, managing editors in this field—who are notoriously pressed for time—will grossly underestimate the amount of time needed to edit a book manuscript. Because their time is at a premium, managing editors may only briefly glance through the manuscript before passing it on for copyediting. More than once I've been told by a managing editor, "This manuscript I'm sending is in good shape and requires a light edit." However, when I've received such a manuscript and actually begun editing it, I've soon discovered that major developmental editing in some cases is necessary. Always beware of a manuscript another editor deems "in good shape." If it sounds to good to be true, it often is; so in my view, it's always better to set your fees hourly. Otherwise, you may receive a lump-sum payment that is disproportionate to your time and effort spent editing and polishing the manuscript.

Working Pro Bono

If the thought of working without pay turns your stomach, take an antacid and think again. Yes, you are starting your own business to be your own boss, and you hope to earn a good living. But you shouldn't run the other way as soon as the topic of providing your services pro bono arises. After all, you never know where or to whom such assignments will lead you. Pro bono work can be a great opportunity for you to build on your portfolio of work samples, especially if you lack samples in a specific area, for instance, corporate communications, advertising, or public relations and marketing.

Case Example 1

When I lived in a suburban Baltimore neighborhood—one of the oldest in the community—organizers there began an association dedicated to communitywide improvement and beautification projects. I volunteered to serve on the association's board of directors and had the opportunity to design, write, and coordinate the production of all its publications, such as newsletters, fliers, brochures, and reports.

After a year of serving on the board, I moved to a more rural area in Maryland. Had I stayed in my previous neighborhood, and continued serving on the board for the community association and doing pro bono work, I probably would have gained additional valuable business contacts and perhaps acquired even more paid editorial assignments. Why? Because by volunteering my time and services, I established contacts with important community leaders, local government officials, and representatives of the local media. Don't automatically disregard pro bono work as a waste of time because there is no payment involved. The payoff could come in forms other than monetary recompense.

Establishing Your Work Space

When it's time to think about where you should establish your work space, you'll want to keep a few practicalities in mind.

Be Budget Conscious

At your business' start-up, you don't even need an entire room dedicated to your home office, although such an arrangement will help you earn a full tax deduction for a home office. Many people who start their own businesses sink thousands of dollars into completely furnishing and equipping their home offices with the latest gadgets and accessories they "must have" in order to run their businesses. You can spend a lot of money fixing up your office and start your business right away in the red, but do you really want to? I started with a typewriter at my kitchen table and later purchased a word processor, and then a computer, and eventually converted a spare bedroom into an office. I've also heard of industrious consultants improvising a desktop by using a large piece of glass or an old door placed across two file cabinets because they had no funds to pay for a desk. Be budget conscious at start-up, and remember that your initial office setup is only temporary.

As your business grows, you may want to redecorate a spare bedroom, renovate a garage loft, or remodel a basement family room and designate it as your office. In time, you even may consider moving your office outside of your home and participate in a shared-office-space arrangement that's a growing trend among many self-employed individuals. In this type of arrangement, an office complex rents space to a variety of business owners, and the renters pool and share expenses for a receptionist, coffeemaker, photocopier, fax machine, courier services, and so on.

Be Comfortable and Productive

Establishing a space that's conducive to creativity and productivity is essential. You'll need lots of light and quiet, so choose an area that's well lit, comfortable, and peaceful. You don't, for example, want to set up your home office in a cold basement with poor or inadequate overhead lighting or in one that receives little or no natural light. Likewise, you don't want your office near distracting noises, such as an air-conditioning or heating unit, that will divert your attention and break your concentration. You won't get much accomplished if you feel uncomfortable in or distracted by your surroundings.

Be Aware of Childcare Needs

If you need absolute silence to complete your work, as I do, and you have babies, toddlers, or preschoolers, you may want to consider having someone come to your home and occupy your children so that you can have uninterrupted blocks of working time. Or, you may want to send your children for care provided outside your home. As my daughter's pediatrician pointed out to me, "If she knows you're in the house, you're going to be interrupted." For more ideas about working at home when you have infants or preschoolers, check out the book *Working at Home While the Kids Are There, Too* (see Suggested Readings).

Purchasing Office Furniture, Equipment, and Supplies

To have your editorial consulting business up and running efficiently, there are some purchases that you'll need to make right away. A conservative estimate of what you'll need to spend initially is $3,000 to $5,000. If you are starting completely from scratch, meaning you do not have the essentials of a home office (i.e., home computer, printer, fax, telephone, desk, and chair) you could spend twice this initial amount. But, again, the question you need to ask yourself is, Do I really want and need to start my business that much in the red?

Some equipment and supplies that you'll need to run your business must be purchased immediately, whereas other less-pertinent items can be placed on your "wish list" for purchase at a later date when funds are more readily available. Consider shopping flea markets and yard sales, visiting scratch-and-dent warehouses, or scanning classified ads for used office equipment and furniture. Gently used items at bargain prices can help keep your start-up costs down.

The following sections are lists of essential home office furniture, equipment, and supplies that you will need for your editorial consulting business. Items with an asterisk (*) indicate less-crucial items that you will not need immediately in order to run your business. You may want to keep a running checklist of these items in your business start-up journal; note the items you already have on hand and those you do not and will need to acquire. Then, you can quickly assess and set a budget for those items you lack.

Furniture

- Desk or work table

- Ergonomic chair

- File cabinets*

- Bookshelves*

Equipment

- Computer with industry-standard word-processing software (e.g., Microsoft Word)

- Bookkeeping and virus-scanning software (e.g., *Quicken, Norton Anti-Virus*)

- Laser printer

- Modem and on-line service for Internet access, e-mail, and research

- Zip drive or tape backup system for backing up hard drive

- Fax machine or access to one (some projects will require you to have a separate fax with more capabilities than a computer's built-in fax provides)

- Dedicated business telephone line* (you can get by with one telephone line initially, but it's best to have another line devoted to your business calls, for professionalism as well as tax purposes)

- Telephone and answering machine

- Copy machine or access to one (or your fax machine may have copying capabilities)

- Cellular telephone* (you can probably get by without one at first, but as your clientele expands, a cell phone is handy when you're stuck in traffic and clients are waiting for you or when you're between client meetings and one runs late)

- Mini-cassette tape recorder* (essential for special-assignment writing when interviews are required or for client meetings when project requirements are discussed)

Supplies

- Standard desktop supplies (e.g., pens, pencils, highlighters, electric sharpener, stapler, staples, paper clips, Rolodex, desk calendar, incoming/outgoing desktop trays, tape and dispenser, calculator, glue sticks, scissors, legal pads, Post-It pads, Post-It flags)

- Padded mailing envelopes or manuscript boxes

- Diskettes and diskette organizer

- High-quality laser printer paper

- High-quality fax paper

- File folders (manila and Pendaflex) and labels

- Static-free dust covers for computer and printer (to promote longevity)

- Stamps (purchase two rolls at first, to eliminate extra trips to the post office)

- Stationery (you don't need to spend a fortune on a professional printer to design and print your business letterhead and stationery; try some of the laser printer stationery available at office supply stores and create your own with your computer to keep costs down)

  - Business cards

  - Letterhead (for proposals, correspondence, invoices, rate sheets)

  - Envelopes

  - Resumes

  - Fliers

  - Brochures

  - Return address/mailing labels

  - Thank you notes (for client referrals and new client business)*

  - Holiday greeting cards*

Miscellaneous Expenses

- Portfolio for work samples (this simply can be a plastic three-ring binder with protective plastic sleeves displaying your work)

- Briefcase (for transporting manuscripts and other materials to and from client meetings)

- Daytimer

- Dues for professional organizations*

- Subscriptions to trade magazines and newsletters*

- Bank fees for business checking account (i.e., account maintenance fees, imprinted business checks)

Reference Books

Another supplies-related expense that you'll face immediately is editorial reference books. New hardback editions of some of these books can be quite costly, but a few basic up-to-date references for your bookshelf are crucial from the outset, such as the following:

- *Bartlett's* or *The Oxford Dictionary of Quotations*

- *The Chicago Manual of Style*

- *Electronic Styles: A Handbook for Citing Electronic Information* or *The Columbia Guide to Online Style*

- *Facts in a Flash: A Research Guide for Writers*

- Strunk and White's *Elements of Style*

- *Harbrace College Handbook* (or audiotapes covering grammar and usage, such as The Princeton Review *Grammar Smart* series)

- *Roget's Super Thesaurus*

- *Webster's Collegiate Dictionary*

As you discover your editorial niche in a particular field (e.g., government, law, medicine, psychology), you'll want to invest in references that apply to and are used in that field, including the following:

- *The American Medical Association Manual of Style: A Guide for Authors and Editors*

- *Associated Press Stylebook and Libel Manual*

- *Scientific Style and Format: The Council of Biology Editors (CBE) Manual for Authors, Editors, and Publishers*

- *Government Printing Office Style Manual*

- *Publication Manual of the American Psychological Association*

- *A Uniform System of Citation*

- *Dorland's* or *Stedman's Medical Dictionary*

- *Physicians' Desk Reference*

- The Merck Index

- Other industry-specific dictionaries and references listing abbreviations, acronyms, terminology, or style points

Financing Your Start-Up Expenses

To finance all of your business start-up expenses, you have several options. You can systematically save in advance, charge on credit cards (but this can be a dangerous option, putting your business in the red right away), borrow from family members or friends, or apply for small-business loans. However, applying for business loans can be tricky and time consuming, particularly if you are the sole income earner in your household. Because at start-up you will not have any proof of your steady income and net profits as a consultant, some banks may not be willing to provide loans because you are considered a financial risk. If yours is a duel-income household, and you have your partner's full-time salary to rely on, a bank may be less likely to consider you a financial risk. It's best to thoroughly check out your bank's loan policies well in advance to avoid disappointments and unwelcome last-minute surprises at loan-processing time. You may even want to consult your tax advisor for a referral of banks that offer a variety of business loans or to determine if you even really require a loan. There are also some government loan programs for which small-business owners may qualify, particularly women. You can obtain details about such programs (e.g., small business assistance for women) from your local office of the Small Business Administration.

TIP!

If at all possible, avoid applying for any type of loan, business or personal, at start-up. I advocate being conservative with spending at business start-up. Why? If you immediately put your business in the red, you take on the additional burden of being able to meet your loan payments, even if your clientele is not well established. Once again, ask yourself if you really want that kind of financial pressure at the beginning stages of your business, when you'll need to focus your energies on finding and keeping good clients. Although some attractive loan programs may be available to you at start-up, I'm in agreement with my CPA, who advises holding off on applying for loans until your business is better established and running smoothly—and profitably.

Case Example 2

My business was up and running for six years when my husband and I decided to move. When it came time to apply for the mortgage loan, I had no idea about the time-consuming documentation process that awaited me because I was self-employed. Although I had steady business from a core group of clients, the bank needed proof and confirmation from each one. During the application process, I had to write the loan committee, providing them detailed documentation of my clients, projects I was working on that had yet to be invoiced, expected income from those projects, and copies of checks received for jobs recently completed and invoiced. In addition, I had to contact each client and request a letter confirming how long I had worked for each one and stating the client's anticipated need for my assistance as an independent contractor in the years ahead. This was an extremely time-consuming and stress-filled task. Be prepared for this time-intensive documentation effort when applying for business loans or any type of personal loan for mortgages, home equity, vehicles, and so on. Keep clients' payment records up-to-date and in a safe place for easy accessibility, and give clients as much advance notice when possible if you should need them to provide correspondence confirming work assignments and requisites for your services.

Confronting Unexpected Disasters

Inevitably, during the course of your day-to-day business operations, you will confront business-related disasters, large or small. Always be prepared for disasters—especially computer problems—to strike at the most inopportune moments because they will.

The most bothersome and frustrating setbacks are technical glitches related to your computer hardware or software. Problems with either one of these can cost you hours or even days of lost editorial time—your livelihood now—and that translates to unpaid time.

Oh No, Not a Fatal Error

In 11 years of running my editorial consulting business, I've had two major computer problems and one not-so-major printer problem, and I consider myself blessed. The first computer problem ensued when a client asked me to coordinate a writing and editorial project that involved compiling and editing the work of six hospital administrators, each of whom was working with a different word-processing software package. At the time, I was working with an older version of Microsoft (MS) Word; however, the majority of the administrators of this top-notch, world-renowned hospital worked with outdated word-processing programs.

I labored many hours converting and compiling the administrators' documents into one huge MS Word file, and early on the project proceeded smoothly, for the most part. There were some symbols and text that were not well converted or incorporated into MS Word, which resulted in some rewriting and reformatting of the manuscript. I had been working on the manuscript, which was an in-depth proposal for a state awards program, for approximately five weeks, meeting with and interviewing administrators, coordinating their manuscripts, and incorporating all of their revisions and additions into the text. Finally, it was time to make the final edits for consistency throughout the manuscript, to proofread it, to save it to disk, and to print out a hard copy for delivery to the client the next day. I had just finished spell checking and saving the final version to disk when my monitor went to black and flashed a "fatal error" message across the screen. There is nothing that stops the heart so readily or induces dread and fear so dramatically as seeing this message displayed across your computer when your are facing a critical deadline. "No, no," I begged my computer, "not now." But there was nothing that could be done in this instance. The fatal error message translated to a crashed hard drive, and there was no retrieving anything from my computer again. Luckily, fate was on my side; earlier that same week, I had backed up all of my current editorial projects to floppy disks, so those projects were still intact and I could later retrieve them once a new hard drive and software had been reinstalled. However, I was out of business for two days until I could purchase a new hard drive and find someone who could help me install it, as well as reload all of my work-related software.

I was doubly lucky that I had a client who was patient and understanding about technical problems. I had saved two copies of the updated document to disk, one of which I had given to the client. When I called and explained to her what had happened, she remained calm and upbeat and then advised me that I could work on-site at one of the spare computers in her department to make any additional last-minute changes to the document.

The lessons I learned from this event were invaluable. Business-related disasters strike when you least expect them, so be prepared and adaptable. It cost me several hundred dollars for a new hard drive and two days of lost editing time, but much more would have been at stake if I had not backed up that particular editorial project, as well as all of my others. Not only would I have irretrievably lost work and income, but I probably would have lost clients as well.

TIP!

Always back up your work regularly onto diskettes, and back up your entire computer system to a zip drive or tape system so that you can retrieve everything whenever disaster strikes.

Oh No, Not a Virus

A second computer-related problem came when a publisher client sent a manuscript to me on disk. Included on the disk was a virus that obliterated my computer's boot-up commands. So, once again, I was all set to work and I was staring at a blank screen and unable to get into or out of a locked-up computer system. Because at that time my computer did not have a virus-scanning program, this incident cost me a half-day's lost work until I could find someone to walk me through the steps of reinstalling my system disk so my computer could be up and running smoothly again. I, again, was lucky at the time this particular technical problem arose because I had two computers (I was in the process of transitioning all of my editorial projects from my old computer to a newer system), and that's exactly what I needed to resolve the problem. After using my older system to copy a series of boot-up commands to a disk and then placing the disk into the new system, I was able to restore the new system to working order. If I did not have access to a second computer at that time, I probably would have lost more than just a half-day's worth of editing time.

After I resolved this technical problem, I also promptly contacted my client and advised him to inform all staff editors to check their computers. Because I had worked on-site for this particular client, I was aware that all of the editors worked from a shared network system. The staff editors constantly sent work to editorial freelancers and graphics contractors, who were also at risk of getting the same virus, which could have had far-reaching consequences for everyone involved. The client was not only apologetic but also appreciative that I had alerted him to the problem. A simple check of the client's shared computer network revealed that indeed a virus was traveling throughout the network.

TIP!

Invest in an up-to-date virus-scanning software package and *always* scan foreign disks before copying them to your hard drive. Computer viruses from your clients' systems can be spread unintentionally, but you can easily prevent them from entering your own system if you are careful about scanning any disk before copying it.

Oh No, Not the Printer

Another not-so-devastating technical problem developed with my six-year-old laser printer, another essential editor's tool. I noticed that my laser printer, an older but reliable model by Packard Bell, was slowly developing poor-quality printouts over time. Some days I'd print out drafts that were completely black on the top third of the page; other drafts were fuzzy and gray throughout; still others had horizontal lines occurring every inch or two down the page.

To resolve these problems, I needed to replace the printer's drum unit, which cost about $300 at that time. The money was not an issue, but there were no local computer dealers who carried the part for my printer. I had to call an out-of-state dealer for delivery of the new drum unit. The part arrived within two days, but for those two days I could print no hard copies. Again, as fate would have it, I was working at that time on a book-editing project; therefore, I did not need to make hard copies of the manuscript, since I was working with disks only and hard copies of the manuscript were not being exchanged between the client and me. Still, I had to wait two days before I could print out correspondence and invoices.

TIP!

Always be prepared in advance for times when your computer equipment, printer, fax, or copier may require service or replacement parts. Know the dealers in your area who supply parts and services, or find reliable out-of-state dealers who can ship parts in a timely manner so that you can avoid work delays.

Dealing with Nonpaying Clients

Another source of frustration you may encounter during the course of running your own business derives from nonpaying clients. More often than not, this issue arises when you are working one-on-one with an individual as a client, not a company. Because the accounting departments of your business clients have legal guidelines and regulations that they must follow and meet in paying vendor invoices, payments sometimes may be processed later than you might expect, but they will not be left unpaid.

For any client who does not pay your invoice on time, say within 30 to 90 days, my best advice is to be patient and persistent. Keep following up your initial invoice with copies that have "payment overdue" boldly stamped across them. If that notation does not get your client's immediate attention or elicit a telephone call and sincere apology from the offending party, you may have to make some telephone calls to the client yourself, particularly when more than 90 days elapse.

Be advised, however, that some companies pay independent contractors and vendors on a quarterly basis only. Other larger national or international companies may be required to submit all contractor invoices through a home office not located in your region, which also can result in delayed payments. You may want to verify with your clients, in advance, what their standard practices are regarding payment of invoices.

In the time I've been running my business, I have never had an invoice that went unpaid, and I have had to send payment overdue notices to only three clients. Again, two of those three clients were individual authors with whom I was working one on one; the other was a large advertising agency that had to submit my invoice to a home office in Ohio, and I eventually received payment—nearly 100 days after I issued my invoice.

Dealing with Rush Assignments

Rush assignments bring their own brand of stress and frustration to the editorial consultant. You'll encounter rush assignments frequently when working with publishers of books and journals, simply because of the notoriously short turnaround times in their production schedules. You also will come across rush projects when working with corporate clients because, invariably, some management type sits on a project far too long and then suddenly realizes a deadline looms and it's time to contract for outside assistance at the eleventh hour.

Determining Rush Status

Always be clear about whether or not an assignment is considered "rush," and don't be intimidated by the rush scenario. Judging a rush-status project becomes crystal clear to you once you've dealt with a variety of clients and you've become comfortable in your business dealings. After you have discussed many different types of editorial assignments with many different types of clients, you definitely will acquire a "feel" for those assignments that can be deemed rush. Some clients will state openly that their projects are running behind schedule and they are therefore rush. Others will not be so forthcoming. Be prepared to question clients about turnaround times. Also, be prepared to explain to clients that your fees differ for rush assignments. Some may say it does not matter what your fees are because they need your services in a hurry, whereas others may balk immediately once the issue of a higher fee is discussed and back down, saying, "Well, we don't really need this in a rush" and "I can probably get the deadline extended."

Determining Your Rush Fee

If clients are willing to pay higher fees for rush assignments, you'll have to devise a fair policy for determining that fee. Once you have discussed and agreed upon a rush assignment fee with your client, always immediately send a follow-up letter documenting the project you discussed, explaining how you determine your rush fee, and estimating hours and cost to complete the job.

There are some options in determining a reasonable rush assignment fee:

- You can charge a flat fee based on your regular fee at time-and-a-half or double time (e.g., your flat fee for copyediting a technical manuscript is $35 per hour and your rush fee is $52.50 or $70, respectively).

- You can charge your regular hourly rate for the first 40 hours and then time-and-a-half or double time for any time spent working beyond those 40 hours to meet the rush deadline (e.g., Your flat fee for editing a nontechnical trade book is $25 per hour for 80 hours or two 40-hour workweeks, but your client wants it turned around in 50 hours. You charge the client $25 per hour for the first 40 hours and $37.50 or $50, respectively, for the remaining 10 hours spent meeting the rush deadline.).

- You can charge a percentage, perhaps 10% or 15%, above your regular hourly rate (e.g., your flat fee for editing a technical manual is $40 per hour and you bill the client $44 or $46 per hour, respectively for a rush assignment).

Depending on the type of editorial assignment and stringency of the rush deadline, I've tried each one of these billing methods. None of my clients has so far objected to any one of these methods for determining rush fees, and, in fact, several have voiced their opinion that each arrangement is fair.

When working with established clients who provide you with a consistent workload, you may even consider giving them somewhat of a price break for rush assignments, particularly if they are budget conscious (and most are). After you prepare your invoice for a rush fee, you may want to deduct a small percentage from the total amount due, perhaps 5% to 10%, as a professional courtesy. If you know your client well, and you enjoy working with each other, you will be able to negotiate a fair deal that satisfies everyone.

When accepting and handling rush assignments, you'll need to work efficiently and intelligently because the stress of meeting rush deadlines can lead directly to the next two work-related problems, namely, conflicting client obligations and burnout. Discussions of these issues follow in the next two sections.

Dealing with Conflicting Client Obligations

When you are working on multiple client projects and deadlines overlap, either because of rush status or just plain coincidence, you can handle these projects in one of three ways:

1. You can accept projects with simultaneous deadlines and eventually try to get deadlines extended on some less-pertinent projects, if necessary.

2. You can subcontract one or more projects, or portions of the project, to another editorial consultant who has the time to complete the work (this option can be time consuming, especially if you do not know editorial professionals who can back you up at a moment's notice, because you will need to screen and train someone whose work you do not know well).

3. You can reject lower-paying assignments and refer clients to another editorial professional who can assist.

Being honest with all of your clients is the best policy when deadlines coincide. After you have been running your business for several years, you will develop a keen sense for what you are able to accomplish. You won't need to jump at every project that comes your way and accept it, no matter how nerve wracking the task. You will become more discerning about taking on some editorial assignments as time goes on, and there will be times when you simply must reject certain projects. You should never be afraid to do so. Clients respect your professionalism when you are honest and straightforward. They would rather have you tell them, "My plate is full right now, and I won't be able to accept another project at the moment," rather than accepting the assignment and failing to meet the deadline or doing a slipshod job.

On a number of occasions, when I've realized overlapping deadlines, I have called clients and explained that I have multiple projects going and have asked for a two- or three-day extension on their original deadline. In every instance, these clients have thanked me for notifying them as soon as possible and then have obliged my request. Always make it a habit to contact your clients immediately and give them as much advance notice as possible when you determine that you need additional time to meet a deadline. Professional courtesy extended to your clients is always a smart policy.

On-Site Work Opportunities

Throughout the course of running your editorial consulting business, you may have opportunities to work on-site with some of your clients. You will need to weigh the advantages and disadvantages of making this type of commitment. I've worked on-site for a number of my clients while still accepting less-time-consuming editorial projects from others so that I would not have to lose or drop core clientele. If an on-site consulting opportunity will provide you with invaluable experiences that supplement your editorial background, resume, and portfolio samples, by all means do it. But should you accept an on-site opportunity for an extended length of time, be prepared to contact all of your clients and inform them about your availability during that time frame.

One of the greatest advantages of working on-site for a client for an extended period is the reliable source of income that you'll have during that time. Although that may seem attractive—especially if your income has been sporadic for some time—remember there also will be some drawbacks. The costs to you need to be considered, in terms of time spent commuting to your client's office, lost income from other clients' projects that you may have to reject as you work on-site, and lost personal time as you catch up on mounding paperwork and other daily duties related to running your business. Once you have committed to working on-site for a client, remember that such an opportunity limits the time you'll have available to attend to other urgent matters, including those pertaining to your other clients, your business, and yourself.

TIP!

Before accepting an offer to work on-site, consult your certified public accountant (CPA) for information about documenting travel and other client-related expenses while working on-site. Depending on the circumstances, working on-site for a client for an extended length of time may affect your consultant status and tax deductions. Be certain to discuss any on-site arrangements with your CPA for guidance and advice.

Case Example 3

A prominent Boston-based publisher approached me when it needed a Baltimore-area editor to coordinate a book for one of the departments of a prestigious teaching hospital. I was advised the project would take approximately two years to complete, working on it full-time or 40 hours per week. After discussing the details and requirements for this book, and meeting with several of the department personnel responsible for writing and producing the book, I began to get a clear picture of what the project would entail. The budgeted hourly rate for the assignment was $16 per hour—before taxes.

At that time, I had about six years' experience in running my business, and I knew from my discussions with representatives of the publisher and the hospital that much more work would be involved than what they had described during our initial meetings. I attempted to negotiate for a higher and fairer hourly rate for the work that would be involved, but I discovered the budget was set and there was no room for adjustment. Because the project necessitated organizing and coordinating the work of nearly a dozen authors, including coordinating meetings and manuscript review sessions with all the authors, writing, typing, copyediting, conducting literature searches, coordinating and incorporating multiauthor revisions, and proofreading, I knew the hourly pay was disproportionate to the work that needed to be done to bring the manuscript to completion. I politely declined the opportunity, although it would have been an impressive project to add to my book-publishing portfolio.

From experience, I was aware that projects involving multiple authors are tremendously time consuming. I also realized that I would have lost time and money by traveling to and from the hospital, paying parking garage fees or meters, and coordinating schedules among nearly a dozen contributors and myself. In addition, I would have had to dedicate two years, full-time, to one editorial project, at the expense of neglecting my other clients and possibly losing them for good. The potential headaches involved in the project quickly became evident.

In time, I discovered I made a wise business decision in rejecting the assignment. About two months later, one of my established book-publishing clients contacted me and asked if I would assist as an on-site project editor during the upcoming year. I readily accepted that offer after negotiating a much fairer on-site hourly rate than the one I had recently been offered by the Boston-based publisher. As it turned out, working on-site for my established publisher-client, as needed, was more beneficial to my business than working with a new, prestigious client. During the time I spent as an on-site project editor for my established client, I learned even more about book publishing and production, I still was able to accept editorial work from other clients, and I was able to build a well-rounded book-publishing portfolio by editing and coordinating numerous books over the course of 14 months, rather than focusing on only one book project for nearly two years.

Dealing with Burnout

When taking on multiple, rush, or on-site editorial assignments, always be realistic about what you can accomplish. As I previously mentioned, at first, you will be tempted to accept every challenge that comes your way. However, once your business has been up and running for a while, you won't feel so desperate to say "yes" to everything. Once you've established your core group of clients, you will have to be selective with your workload so that you won't burn out. If you are a one-person operation and have several clients, you must accept the fact that you simply cannot accomplish all of your editorial projects and run your business in a 40-hour workweek. Get organized, set priorities, and work efficiently. There are not enough hours in the day, let alone a week, for one person to meet all of these business-related obligations. If you do attempt to be everything to everyone while trying to run your business, you'll soon find yourself overwhelmed, and you aren't an effective consultant when you spread yourself too thin.

Know When to Ask for Help

The early realization that you cannot work a full 40-hour week for each one of your clients, while tending to smooth business operations as well as family obligations, will stave off mounding stress. As your business grows and you become busier, juggling multiple deadlines and clients, realize that some sector of your life surely stands to suffer if you attempt to do more than your sole-business-owner status permits. Know your boundaries and beware of overextending yourself to demanding clients in order to prevent unwanted, untoward side effects in other realms of your life—especially your physical and mental health, family and home life, or core clientele relationships. Some clients, when they come to know your work and rely on your assistance, may begin to think of you as "all theirs." If you start to notice this attitude developing among one or more of your clients, you'll need to remind them, gently, that as a consultant you work for yourself and have not just one client but other clients to assist as well.

When multiple deadlines loom for an ever-increasing workload, and you do not know other editorial consultants who can assist, you will have to learn to say "no" to some assignments. In your consulting career, you eventually will come to the conclusion that it's better to reject some projects. It took me nearly seven years to learn to refuse certain nonlucrative editorial assignments. As I mentioned previously, when you are just starting your business, you will be hungry for work and ready to take any assignment, to meet any challenge. But as you mature as a business owner, you will learn to recognize, and become more selective in accepting, the kinds of projects you truly enjoy working on and to decline those projects that are less desirable.

If you do need the backup of another editor, it's possible either to work with him or her on part of the assignment or to refer the client directly to the other editor. Depending on how comfortable you are with either of those arrangements, you may want to consider a payment agreement with the other editor. This agreement can be handled in one of two ways: 1) you pay the other editor a percentage of the total income from the assignment upon completion of his or her duties, or 2) the other editor pays you a certain percentage for your referral if he or she completes the assignment in its entirety for your client. Either option works well when both editors are in agreement and each knows the other's editorial work and business practices.

Be careful when working with other consulting editors, though. I've heard many horror stories about editors who have subcontracted heavy workloads to others and ended up regretting it. Either the other editor's work was substandard and deadlines were missed, or the first editor ended up in a legal battle trying to recoup his or her "finder's percentage" for the subcontracted work. When my workload has gotten extremely heavy, it has always been my policy simply to prioritize and reject nonlucrative projects. I just don't want the headaches of managing others' work, and I, like many other editors, don't want to lose the control of completing an assignment according to my clients' standards. Involving others is a choice you'll have to consider many times throughout the course of running your own business, and you'll have to do what feels most comfortable for you, based on the relationship you have with your client and on the type of editorial project.

In addition, if you reject a project and refer your client to another editor, be certain the other editor is professional and reliable. Otherwise, you may discover that your client does not approach either one of you for work again.

Case Example 4

I had the opportunity two work on-site for two of my clients during an overlapping time frame for six months. Three days a week, I commuted to and from Washington, D.C., to assist a book publisher as an on-site project editor, and the other two days, I commuted to and from a Baltimore-based advertising/marketing agency. Each client was aware that I was working on-site with the other. Juggling two on-site work assignments for two different clients can be a challenge, but it can be done if you have flexible clients who understand that you work not only with them, but also with other clients. At all times, be honest about your availability to assist and clients will be willing to accommodate your schedule, as long as you are conscientious about your clients' needs and good at what you do.

Build Recreation Time into Your Schedule

You've probably heard of endorphins, those feel-good hormones released after vigorous exercise. Don't discount the benefits that exercise has on the mind, body, and soul. Schedule some heart-healthy activity into your daily schedule; write it in your daytimer and keep the appointment. If your workload prohibits you from an uninterrupted 45-minute or hour-long workout, you can take three 15- to 20-minute walks throughout your workday and still reap the physical and mental benefits of exercise. Walking is one of the best and easiest exercises you can do, and if you still believe you can't possibly leave your office, then take a few minutes throughout the day to do some stretching, especially concentrating on the neck, shoulders, arms, back, and legs, where tension quickly lodges.

Taking time for yourself is crucial to your physical and mental well-being. An unhealthy or—even worse—a hospitalized consultant is of little use to clients. One of the best ways to prevent and relieve stress and burnout as an editor is to schedule a vacation each year. You may not be able to take an extended vacation during the first few years of business start-up, but you can at least take a weekend to unwind and clear your head. Once you have established your business and you know the ebbs and flows of your workload, you can schedule one or more weeklong vacations to obtain the maximum benefits of their refreshing and restorative qualities.

Chapter 6

Step 6: Cultivating and Maintaining Your Client Base

You have probably heard the advice thousands of times that networking can get you the job you really want. Nowhere does that piece of advice ring truer than in the day-to-day efforts of running your own business. Networking and word-of-mouth referrals have contributed to nearly 60% to 70% of my editorial business. The other 30% to 40% of my business has come from a combination of cold calling, distributing marketing packets about my services to companies that I've researched, and listing my name and services in the membership directories of professional organizations that I've joined.

Never Burn Bridges

Although "never burn your bridges" is somewhat of a cliché in the business world, this is another valid bit of advice to remember once you are on your own. Always try to maintain contact and friendships with colleagues and supervisors from your previous full-time positions. These contacts can be some of your most helpful resources and allies when you are just starting your business.

You really don't need to start your business as some sort of covert operation; tell everyone you know. If you're planning to leave a full-time job and you've already given notice, explain your plans to your superiors. You may even get an on-the-spot offer for contractual work from your soon-to-be ex-employer.

I stayed in touch with many of my former coworkers and managers from full-time positions I had held, and they helped me build my business during its initial stages of development. As an undergraduate student, I had an internship with one company that later became one of my first full-time employers. Although I had left employment with that company for nearly six years before starting my own business, I stayed in contact with my supervisors there. Early on in my business, one of the vice presidents and a manager, who both were aware of my start-up plans, contacted me and discussed an on-site work assignment when their department became short-staffed and they were conducting a personnel search. They needed an interim person to complete various assignments, and since I had previously held the job and was familiar with the responsibilities, they requested my assistance. I was able to step in immediately to help out, and they were able to avoid spending a lot of time searching for and training a temporary employee. I sat down with my former employer, and now a new client, to negotiate a part-time on-site work schedule and still had time to assist my other clients with their editorial projects.

I've also had colleagues from previous jobs call me and ask for editorial assistance. When I worked at a Baltimore-based public relations/advertising agency, one of my colleagues eventually was offered a new position as a vice president of marketing with a local financial institution. When she was in her new job for several months, she contacted me for contractual work on her new employer's publications. After working with her on this company's publications for about a year, I became familiar with the related duties for each publication. I became well acquainted with members of the marketing staff and other departments within that company, and I was accustomed to working closely with them. When this same colleague needed an extended medical leave of absence, the marketing director approached me and requested that I temporarily assume the vice president's duties on-site because I was already familiar with her publications and responsibilities.

Another colleague of mine and I crossed paths when I was in business eight years. When I first began my business, I freelanced as a news and feature writer for a publication that he edited. The editor eventually left his position, and we lost touch for nearly eight years. One day I noticed his name in the classified section of the local newspaper. He had recently begun his own publication and needed editorial assistance. I sent him a letter and a marketing package with updated information about my business, and he contacted me within a week. This editor contacted me immediately because distribution of his start-up regional publication was growing rapidly, and he needed familiar, reliable editorial assistance. After we met, exchanged information about our growing businesses, and discussed possible contractual working arrangements, he offered me two different full-time job opportunities. However, because I had been running my business for nearly 10 years, I was not prepared to accept a full-time position, so I politely declined those opportunities and we agreed on contractual editorial assistance as the need arose.

Each one of these former employers and colleagues proved to be helpful and long-lasting contacts. More than likely, you, too, will have one or more opportunities to work with former colleagues and supervisors when you have your own business, if you previously parted on good terms and if you remained in high professional standing in their eyes.

You never know what type of opportunities await you if you stay in touch with former associates from full-time jobs and your very first clients who eventually move on to new jobs or who start their own businesses. In addition, you probably will be offered a full-time opportunity, at least once, as your clients become familiar with your work and accustomed to your professionalism.

After you have been in business for some time, however, I doubt that such opportunities will seem appealing. In the first few years of running your own business, when money is tight, you may be tempted by the comforts and advantages of a full-time position: steady, reliable income; paid vacation and sick leave; paid health insurance; and other perquisites. I am convinced, though, that if you focus beyond the comforts that a full-time offer seems to provide, you will discover, as I have, that the freedom, variety of editorial assignments and clients, and self-satisfaction you acquire in running your own business all far outweigh the advantages derived working full-time for any one company or person. As Paul and Sarah Edwards—the self-employment experts—explain this shift in thinking, you will have abandoned the "paycheck mentality" and opened yourself to the "ambiguity of opportunity." In other words, the opportunities and possibilities that await you as a self-employed editor become more attractive to you than does a steady paycheck.

Win Word-of-Mouth Referrals

Word-of-mouth referrals or recommendations are another great source for editorial assignments. To obtain these, you'll have to do not just an *okay* job, not just a *good* job, but a *meticulous* job so that your work will be recognized and remembered and you'll be referred to other clients. I had one client, for example, who referred a small advertising agency to me for an on-site editorial stint. While I was there, one staff member left to work for one of the largest, well-known advertising agencies in my state and in North America. I had known for only a brief time the staff member who left, but she passed along information about my editorial business to the powers that be at her new employer, and soon I was receiving calls from some of that agency's staff for editorial assistance.

TIP!

Always remember that the key to getting word-of-mouth referrals is doing a meticulous editing job. Your work inevitably will impress someone, and that person, in turn, will lead you to additional work assignments.

In addition, as I discussed in Chapter 5, do not immediately reject pro bono assignments, such as coordinating a newsletter for your church or preparing a brochure for a nonprofit organization. The experience and client contacts that you gain from pro bono work can be invaluable. Although there is no monetary compensation for the work done, you may be compensated in other ways, such as acquiring additional prospective clients who will pay you for your work or acquiring interesting editorial work that may lead you in a new direction. Just because a certain editorial job offers no remuneration does not mean you should automatically reject it as worthless. You never know where or to whom a particular editorial job or client will lead you. You may even be pleasantly surprised. So, ride the wave and go with the opportunities as they are presented to you.

Make Some Cold Calls

It's a nasty job but somebody's got to do it, and that somebody is you. You inevitably are going to have to make a few cold telephone calls at your business' start-up; there is no way around this task. The best advice I can offer is always speak with a director of communications, public relations, or marketing when dealing with corporate and nonprofit entities, or speak with managing editors if you are contacting publishers. Do not contact personnel or human resources departments. Start at the top and attempt to reach and speak with the decision makers of a particular company. If you cannot speak directly with that person, then speak with his or her assistant or an associate director or editor.

Initially, you'll simply be inquiring about whether or not the company or publisher contracts with freelancers and consultants to assist with publications. If the contact informs you that the company does use the services of independent contractors, ask if you may forward information about your services and request the appropriate contact's name, professional title, and address. Then, compose a cover letter, compile your marketing packet, and mail it off within a day or two of your initial telephone call. Be careful and meticulous with your cover letter and marketing materials because these introduce you and your services and leave a lasting first impression. Double-check the spelling of the contact's name, professional title, and address for accuracy. Nothing turns off potential clients more rapidly than a sloppy editor who misspells contacts' names or uses incorrect or outdated professional titles. Also be certain that the contents of your cover letter and marketing packet are error free. Showcase your professionalism from the outset when contacting potential clients.

TIP!

I've found that the best time to place cold calls to prospective clients is Friday morning, at start of business, around 9 a.m. or 10 a.m., or in the afternoon, just before close of business, between 2 p.m. and 3 p.m. I'm not sure if the end of the workweek makes some contacts you'll speak with more buoyant and open, but I have discovered that most decision makers seem less stressed and more willing to speak with consultants on Fridays.

Be persistent with companies that you'd like to work with but do not have a response from after six to eight weeks. After you have mailed your marketing packet to the appropriate contact, follow up with a telephone call and request to speak with him or her. Confirm whether or not your contact received the information you forwarded and tell him or her to feel free to call you in the months ahead should your assistance be needed for any editorial projects. If you do not hear from that company, call your contact back in two to three months' time to follow up again. If nothing else, these follow-up calls will keep your name and services in the forefront of your contacts' minds, which may eventually lead to editorial assignments in the not-too-distant future. I adhered to this follow-up procedure with two companies in which I was interested. Although I did not receive work from them immediately, I eventually received calls from their directors of communication requesting my editorial assistance about a year after my initial cold telephone calls to their offices. You may have to expend some effort and energy on cold calling and follow-up calls, but this method can, and usually does, pay off in the future.

Take a Test

Whereas corporate entities will request your resume and any marketing materials you have prepared about your services, most publishers of books and journals will request that you take and pass a sample copyediting and/or proofreading test. Do not be intimidated by such a request. The tests are designed for the benefit of busy managing editors who need to gauge your experience and ability to grasp a particular publisher's editorial guidelines.

As you accumulate editorial experience, you may not need to take tests. Instead, you may be asked to provide a list of books or journals that you've edited, stylebooks you regularly used to complete the editing (e.g., *The American Medical Association Manual of Style: A Guide for Authors and Editors, The Chicago Manual of Style, Government Printing Office Style Manual*), and names of editors who can attest to your work.

I've heard some of my editorial colleagues balk about taking copyediting and proofreading tests: "It's too time consuming," "It's work on speculation that goes unpaid," or "I shouldn't be expected to take a test when I have all kinds of editorial experience." The truth of the matter is, if you refuse to take a test, you could be labeled as difficult to work with and immediately put off a potential client. My advice is to take a test when a managing editor makes such a request. After all, a prospective client has no idea of your editorial capabilities or level of experience. Let a managing editor know that you can meet and may exceed his or her editorial guidelines and expectations.

If you are a seasoned editorial professional when you take a test, it will not seem time consuming or cumbersome to you. Most likely, the test will seem easy because you already will have acquired a well-rounded background and sufficient editorial experience to make you feel at ease demonstrating your skills on paper. Seen from the managing editor's perspective, the test is a helpful aid in weeding out seasoned editors from those who simply designate themselves "editors." There are many individuals lurking out there who claim to be editors but who lack the specific skills and knowledge required in both developmental editing and copyediting.

Demonstrating your editorial skills on a test may lead to immediate assignments and regularly scheduled, ongoing editorial work after you have passed the test. I took several copyediting tests for publishers of scholarly books and journals at the start-up of my business. In each instance, after completing and passing the tests, I've acquired continuous editorial assignments within a span of six to eight weeks.

Prepare a Simple, Informative Marketing Packet

The marketing packet that you send to potential clients will include a cover letter, resume, business card, brochure or flier, and writing or editing samples, if the prospective client requests those. You do not need to spend a lot of money preparing your marketing materials. Nowadays, you can design your own inexpensively on your computer. Office supply stores have coordinating stationery packages that you can buy for about $10. With this small investment, you can purchase a supply of stationery for your letterhead, envelopes, business cards, brochures, fliers, resumes, invoices, and labels. All of your business-related stationery will have a consistent look, and you won't pay a high-priced designer or printer to obtain that look (see Appendix A). You can create basic designs for your stationery with the word-processing software on your computer, and print out your entire supply of stationery on your laser printer at home. Creating and printing your own stationery supply at home affords you cost-saving benefits at start-up. When I began my business 11 years ago, I paid a printer $50 for 500 business cards—nothing else.

The only disadvantage that I have found with these store-bought stationery packages is the stock for business cards and labels, which tends to be a heavier-weight paper than some older-model laser printers can accept and process. I had an older-model laser printer, and when it was time to print out my business cards, they kept jamming my printer. I simply saved my business card template to disk, and found a wonderful local, low-cost printer who took my disk and printed out 100 cards for about $7. Although I incurred an additional expense to print out my business cards, $7 was still more reasonable to me than the $50 I had paid at start-up for a professional printer to select card stock, typeface style, and logo. At that time, the smallest quantity the printer could order was 500, and more than half of those went to waste when I moved and relocated my business.

When you first start your business, you'll be sending out numerous marketing packets as a means of soliciting new clients. Be prepared; have lots of copies compiled and ready to go, so you won't lose time organizing and packaging your materials for each mailing. As your business grows, you won't be sending out your complete marketing packet as frequently as in the beginning. For word-of-mouth referrals, for example, you may need to send only your business card and brochure.

An inexpensive way to keep all of your marketing materials coordinated and nicely displayed is a color-coordinated two-pocket folder that has a business-card holder notched on the front. One editor/publisher I know distributes information about his business using this approach. In the folder, he includes a cover letter, a current copy of the publication, circulation information, and a few clips regarding his business' start-up and successes. Media coverage is another option as an enclosure in your packet, and it is evidence of the level of success you have achieved as a business owner. If your business receives media coverage, it is always a good idea to include copies of newspaper, newsletter, or magazine articles or any blurbs and/or copies of video- and audiotapes used in the broadcast media so that you can proclaim your success to potential clients who are considering your services.

TIP!

Be sure to revise your resume before sending it to potential clients. A consultant's resume differs from a resume you send when seeking full-time employment (an example is shown in Appendix A). At the top of the resume, you still will include your personal information, such as name, address, telephone/fax numbers, and e-mail address. After that information, however, you'll highlight in a bulleted list your areas of specialization, such as editing scholarly works, educational texts, or collateral corporate communications. Choose about three specialties that you would like to focus on during the course of your business operations so that you may interest a wide variety of clients and obtain different types of editorial assignments. On my resume, for example, I list services that apply to publishers of scholarly books and journals; public relations, advertising, marketing, and corporate communications professionals; and publishers of periodicals. After listing your areas of specialization, you'll simply list your full-time positions, education, and any professional organizations to which you belong as a member. (Once you have been in business for some time and have worked for various clients, you will list the clients that you have assisted immediately following the "Areas of Specialization" section. See Appendix A, Fig. 4a) Some of the books included in the Suggested Readings list offer additional guidance in preparing your consultant's resume.

List Your Business in a Directory or Database

Once you have joined one or more professional organizations for editors and writers and have discovered they publish a membership directory, you'll want to take full advantage of this opportunity for free advertising (see Chapter 3 for a complete discussion). Take the time to complete the required paperwork accurately so that your business can be included. Some groups, such as the Editorial Freelancers Association, for example, have quite a detailed list of specialties from which you select and that best describe your services. It may take an hour or two to review and fill out the forms, but it's well worth the time invested—no matter how detailed or tedious the paperwork. You will get telephone calls or e-mails from other members or businesses that need your expertise, and those contacts usually result in paid work. As I mentioned previously, many professional organizations, as a public service, distribute their membership directories locally and nationally to business leaders that frequently use independent editorial contractors. These business leaders have come to rely on the referrals provided in the directories, and once a good working relationship is developed with an editorial referral, they consult the directory again and again.

If you are interested in procuring government contracts, for instance, you also can list your services on *Pro-Net*, the Small Business Administration's (SBA's) on-line database of small businesses. It's free to register your business with *Pro-Net*, and by doing so, you'll reach many contracting officers for the federal government all at once, rather than submitting individual marketing packets. You can access the *Pro-Net* website at <http://pronet.sba.gov>. At this site, you can also explore links to other procurement opportunities, home pages of additional federal agencies, and *Commerce Business Daily,* a publication listing government agencies that are currently soliciting bids for goods and services.

Case Example

I had the opportunity to do editorial work for an international hotel chain because I had listed information about my services in a directory for a professional organization composed of writers and editors. A fellow member, who served as editorial director for the hotel chain, contacted me when she saw that my areas of specialization listed in the directory included editorial work in corporate communications, particularly coordinating and editing newsletters. We met, discussed duties, hourly rate, and availability, and I was contracted on the spot to provide editorial assistance.

Experiment with Paid Advertising

Advertisements

Another inexpensive option for you to get the word out about your business and services is to run a small advertisement in one or more of the trade publications. *Literary Market Place, Publishers Weekly, The Writer, Writer's Digest,* and *Editor & Publisher* are just a few of the better-known publications you can try. You also can contact professional organizations for writers and editors and inquire about the possibility of advertising in their newsletters. You'll have to contact these publications by telephone, check their websites, or get a copy of a current issue to determine current rates for classified ads, but the cost to run a few lines of copy should be minimal and affordable.

Fliers

Creating inexpensive fliers about your services and distributing them by hand to businesses or institutions in your area is another means of advertising your business. You also might want to research and create a mailing list of prospective clients and then distribute the fliers by standard U.S. mail service or bulk rate service if you have ample prospects. Try mailing a flier about your services with all of your correspondence; you never know who might be in need of an editor.

Trade Shows

You might want to consider renting a booth at one of the business trade shows or expositions held in your area each year. In my area, for example, there is a convention for home-based business owners held each fall at the local fairgrounds and another one held during the spring for women business owners. You can call your local fairgrounds or convention center for a listing of upcoming trade shows, or check your local newspaper's business section for a calendar of events. Then, simply contact the sponsoring organizations of these events to determine their fees for renting a space or booth at the show. If you are a member of the sponsoring organization, you may be entitled to a reduced rate to display information about your business.

Websites

Everybody seems to be on the Internet bandwagon these days, promoting their businesses electronically. Electronic advertising, marketing, and promotion may be a consideration for you once you have been in business for some time. But promoting your business and services on the Internet via your own website can be a costly undertaking at start-up.

Since website promotion is a relatively new method for advertising and marketing a business, all the data are not yet in regarding the benefits to the editorial consultant. Many business owners seem to be in a mad rush to establish a presence on the Web, but there remain many unanswered questions, such as

- Is it cost-effective for me to maintain a website at this point in my business?

- Who are the most reliable resources to help me establish and maintain my website?

- Do I really need a website to run my business?

- Do I have the time to tend to and update my website?

Some of my editorial colleagues who have websites say they feel overwhelmed trying to maintain their websites while tending to daily editorial- and business-related responsibilities. One said that she believes she could hire someone full-time just to handle this one aspect of her business. For an editorial consultant who is just starting out, hiring another employee is not an option.

If you simply cannot or do not want to invest the funds, time, and energy in overseeing your own website, you might be able to get your business and services advertised on the World Wide Web by another means. For instance, if you join a professional organization, you may be able to get a listing on its website. Or, if you contact your college's alumni association, you also might be able to list your business and services for free.

There may be other low-cost or no-cost alternatives to Internet advertising. Network with other consultants; contact the SBA,

Chamber of Commerce, or other organizations; or call your alma maters and you may discover some interesting alternatives to footing the entire website bill yourself, such as locating student-intern designers and managers. Website costs can be intimidating for the new business owner, but if you search long and hard enough, they don't have to be.

Before you take the leap into Internet advertising and promotion, talk with as many Web professionals as possible. Technology and tools for designing and maintaining your website are rapidly advancing, so seek professional guidance to stay informed. Websites can be a great option for promoting your editorial business and networking with other editorial professionals (i.e., through links to websites of colleagues, as well as to writing and editorial organizations). There are ways to optimally position your business on the various World Wide Web search engines that will prove advantageous to your Internet presence. Web designers and technicians who know the tricks of the trade can help you get the greatest benefits for your website advertising dollar.

Experiment with Free Publicity

Newspaper, Television, Radio

Finally, you always have the option of seeking free publicity and advertising about your business by getting your name, business' name, and details about your services in print, on television, or on the radio. Any time you have newsworthy information to share about your business, you can write a press release and distribute it to the appropriate editors at some of the big-city daily newspapers, smaller community weekly newspapers and business periodicals, as well as local television and radio stations. If you conduct a seminar or speaking engagement related to your editorial business, you can also prepare a public service announcement about the event for broadcast on radio and television stations.

Workshops and Speaking Engagements

Holding workshops on editing and becoming part of a speakers' bureau are effective methods for establishing your presence in the business community and getting the word out about your services. You may want to start by contacting any of your alma maters to determine if you could hold a workshop, teach a course, or address students about your business. High schools and colleges often hold career planning days when professionals visit and talk about their lines of work and job opportunities in their field. Contact the alumni associations of schools, colleges, and universities you have attended or graduated from to determine their interest.

By staying in touch with your former professors and instructors, you also may be invited to return to their classrooms and have an opportunity to talk about your business—without making a formal offer to do so. Instructors and professors are often interested in having guests throughout the year to speak to their classes on subjects they are currently covering in class. You might even get a kick out of doing such speaking engagements. You'll feel a sense of accomplishment returning to the campus of your alma mater and speaking with a former professor's current group of students, sharing your expertise as a professional and speaking from the other side of the lecturer's podium.

The university I attended, from which I earned both my undergraduate and graduate degrees, has an active career advisory network consisting of alumni association members. This network holds a career planning conference each year on the grounds of the university. Participants attend workshops and meet one-on-one with alumni members who are part of the network. If your college or university offers such opportunities, seek more information and volunteer to take part in these kinds of events. You never know who might attend these events and need your assistance as an editorial expert.

Your local Chamber of Commerce, civic groups (e.g., Kiwanis Club, Lions Club, Rotary Club), and any professional organizations to which you belong are also good contacts because these groups often have a speakers' bureau. Call and inquire if they have a roster of community professionals who speak to their members and if you are eligible to be a part of their speakers' bureau.

Although you may not be paid for leading workshops or being a guest speaker, both opportunities garner free publicity and promotion for your editorial consulting business. Your name and face will become well known in the community where you live and conduct business. Once you have held several workshops or spoken before students and civic groups, you may discover that you are comfortable teaching and sharing your knowledge and expertise. As a natural progression along your career path as an editorial consultant, you might even decide to pursue a career teaching editing courses, another option for increasing your income.

Writing Articles

Writing and submitting articles to local papers, including daily newspapers, community weeklies, regional trade publications, and periodicals of professional organizations, is another means of generating free publicity about your business.

You may want to pitch your ideas to or query the editors of these types of publications first, and then volunteer to write an article or series of articles related to your editorial expertise. Having publishing credits (i.e., clips with your byline) in print materials is good free publicity for you and your business.

Editors of periodicals, especially local ones, are usually eager to work with local talent, and they will appreciate your offer to supply free articles that meet their editorial needs. By taking this initiative, you may get invited to contribute a regular column. You'll then enjoy the double benefit of gaining greater exposure for your business and earning payment for your work.

These are just a few of the most frequently used methods of inexpensive advertising and free publicity you can use to cultivate and maintain your core client base and to spread the word about your services. Over the years, you can try some or all of these techniques to promote your business, attract new clients, and help your editorial consulting business grow and develop, perhaps leading you into new directions you never imagined when you first began your business.

Written Contracts and Verbal Agreements

As clients begin contacting you for editorial assistance, you'll need to consider how you would like to contract with them for your services. Throughout the years, in contracting with my clients for editorial services, I have never used a formal written contract. I suppose that perhaps I have been naïve and have taken chances in all these years of running my business, but verbal agreements, follow-up letters, or proposals have served me well. I have found all of my clients to be honest and ethical in their business practices, and so I have never devised a formal written contract for my services, although some editors may choose to do so. None of my clients has ever asked me for a formal written contract, although some corporate clients have asked me for a one-page proposal detailing scope of services, estimate of hours and cost, and tentative timeline for completion of the assignment.

You may work with some publishing clients who have their own paperwork for you to complete when you return each assignment. They may provide agreement forms and checklists that you will have to fill out, sign, date, and return along with your completed editorial work and invoice. It's good business practice always to oblige clients' requests for timely completion and return of any paperwork they need for their records. Keep copies for your files as well.

If you do want to prepare a written contract for your clients but don't know exactly what to include, contact any of the professional organizations in which you hold membership, the SBA, or Chamber of Commerce for suggestions and help. You also can check their websites for sample contracts. Other good sources to check for help in preparing a written contract are the *Writer's Market* and *National Writers Union Guide to Freelance Rates and Standard Practice* (see Suggested Readings).

Chapter 7

Step 7: Keep Your Business Running Smoothly in the Years Ahead

*O*nce you have established your editorial consulting business and you have systematically taken all of the steps discussed so far, remember the following three commonsense principles to help you keep your business up and running for many years to come:

1. Always do a meticulous job.

2. Always stay in touch with your clients.

3. Always pay your taxes on time.

Do a Meticulous Job

One of the keys to doing a meticulous job as an editor is to keep up with your trade in the years ahead by reading books and articles on writing and editing, and by taking continuing education classes or seminars. From time to time, hone your editing and proofreading skills with exercises found in books or on audiotapes. These steps will contribute to your ability to do a job that's thorough and one that will get you recognized and referred for more editorial jobs as the years unfold.

In this book, I have focused on the practical, step-by-step guidelines you will need to take in starting and maintaining your editorial consulting business. I have not set out to instruct you on the practice of developmental editing or copyediting, and the accompanying minutiae that each of these skills commands, because there are a number of excellent resources already available to you if you need that sort of training. Two of the best books on editing that I have read are Karen Judd's *Copyediting* and Arthur Plotnik's *The Elements of Editing* (see Suggested Readings). Reading resources such as these, familiarizing yourself with stylebooks, and honing your writing and editing skills by doing the practice exercises included in handbooks on grammar, style, and language usage are the groundwork for doing meticulous editing, if you are not already an experienced editor. I highly recommend purchasing and reading these books thoroughly before you start your own business. You will educate yourself about editorial practice and familiarize yourself with standard stylistic guidelines that most industry professionals adhere to and follow.

Knowing standard editorial practices and procedures, and understanding the reasons why you are observing them, is important to your success as a professional editor. Your love of language and reading more than likely have contributed to your interest in the editorial field. Honing these skills through continuous practice will help you stand out from the rest of those so-called editors who are not so interested in all the pesky little details involved in editing, especially copyediting. Your ability to do a thorough job as an editor is what polishes a manuscript to make it shine.

In doing a meticulous editorial job, one caveat applies: do not overedit or change the voice of a writer's work. Follow client-specified guidelines exactly as explained. Do not be overzealous with your red pen or delete button, and never be pompous or self-righteous in queries to the author. There is nothing more off-putting to clients and authors than an editorial consultant who insists that his or her way *only* is the right way. Be flexible. Clients, particularly book publishers, should provide you with any editorial guidelines that stray from the norm. If an author uses a nonstandard approach to his or her piece of writing, you should be advised as to how the manuscript differs from normal editorial guidelines (e.g., an author has capitalized or hyphenated certain terms or phrases, or has a preference for using boldface to introduce new terms and definitions rather than using italics). Know your clients' guidelines and preferences for each manuscript on which you have the opportunity to work, and don't be afraid to ask questions if you are uncertain of those preferences.

In the rare instance that editorial guidelines or stylistic preferences are not provided, ask your clients if it would be acceptable for you to establish a set of stylistic guidelines for their publications. You may come across such a situation when working with some corporate entities, nonprofit groups, or individual authors, for instance. Discuss stylistic options and choices with your client, and create your own style sheet that your clients can refer to and use for future publications (see page 14 for a discussion of style sheets). It is better to settle stylistic issues at the start of a project, rather than beginning your editorial work, making sweeping changes throughout a manuscript, and much later discovering that the changes you made are not what the client preferred. Deadlines can be affected if you put off discussing stylistic issues of which you are unsure. You must develop almost a sixth sense about the amount of editing each client—especially a new one—wants and needs: does the client prefer a light, medium, or heavy edit? Likewise, you'll need to know how much editorial rein you'll have on the manuscript. At the risk of over- or sidestepping your client's wishes, always confirm the best course of action with him or her whenever significant changes need to be made manuscriptwide.

Stylistic divergences from the norm are compromises a managing editor probably has already worked out with an author.

It therefore would be a mistake to go ahead and completely change the manuscript, regardless of your awareness that a certain stylistic deviation is wrong or nonstandard. If you do make sweeping changes without consulting the managing editor first, you risk offending or even angering your client, losing time going back and changing the manuscript to its original format, not getting paid for your work, or getting paid but never getting another job from that client again because you took too heavy an editorial hand to the manuscript. Be cautious and be judicious. When in doubt, always ask the client before proceeding with changes to the manuscript.

TIP!

Meticulous attention given to spelling, grammar, and punctuation is a sound editorial approach with any manuscript. In some instances, that is all you will be required to do. Subjective stylistic changes to format or content, which you think would improve a manuscript, are better discussed early on in your work so that you do not offend an author or editorial client. You do not want your clients labeling you as hard to work with, stubborn, or amateurish.

The skills of a professional editorial consultant should always be improving and evolving. This point is especially important to remember as electronic and print-on-demand publishing grow in the years ahead. What will become industry standard for those modes of publishing may introduce yet another set of stylistic guidelines and principles with which you must be familiar. As a consulting editor, you always must be aware of the trends in publishing and editing.

Classes, seminars, and training in copyediting, proofreading, and developmental writing and editing, as well as continuing computer training, will contribute to your skills and experience. Keep informed of industry trends by reading trade publications, such as newsletters and magazines of professional editorial associations, as well as by reading listserv information and Internet articles targeted to editors. Brushing up or improving on your skills and staying current with editorial standards and trends will help you grow in and stay educated about your trade in the years ahead. Ultimately, honing or adding editorial skills will help your business grow.

Stay in Touch with Clients

There may be times when you inevitably will need to take a break from your editorial work or to reduce your working hours for the short term for one or more of your clients (e.g., when handling simultaneous client obligations or when working on-site for multiple clients). Always remain honest and straightforward with each of your clients. Give clients as much advance notice as possible whenever you feel you need a deadline extension or whenever an editorial assignment will require a greater amount of work than initially estimated.

When you are working on particularly lengthy editorial projects, keep clients apprised of your progress. Depending on which method of communication your client prefers, use reports and memos, e-mail or voice mail messages, or faxes. Remember that an informed client is a happy client. If a client never hears from you regarding your progress or never receives regular updates about your work and ability to meet an approaching deadline, he or she probably will begin to question your professionalism, or lack thereof. Never leave clients wondering what you are doing.

If you will be taking an extended leave from your editorial responsibilities (e.g., to tend to an ill relative, a new infant, or preschool-age children, or for personal medical reasons), request that your clients keep your information on file in the years ahead so that you can resume working with them when you return to your regular schedule of editorial responsibilities. Most clients with whom you have a well-established working relationship are understanding and more than happy to oblige. They may even provide you with smaller editorial assignments or projects with open-ended deadlines that you can complete in your spare time so that you remain actively working with them during the interim.

Pay Your Taxes on Time

One of the best pieces of advice I ever remember receiving was offered at a Small Business Administration seminar. The advice was simple: always pay your taxes *on time*. Know that the Internal Revenue Service will catch up with you if you try to avoid paying, or simply forget to pay, your business taxes. You won't have a business too long if you try to avoid paying Uncle Sam his due share. You do not want to send up any red flags to the federal or local tax authorities because they will catch up with you, possibly through audits or payment overdue notices and tax penalties. If your business is audited or penalized, it could sink into debt before it's had a chance to thrive.

When you receive payment on your invoices to clients, remember to put aside the required amount you will owe in taxes. Do not spend entire paychecks from your clients because approximately one-third of the full amount will be going to county, state, and federal revenue authorities. If you do not send them their portions, you can expect to pay large amounts in back taxes that went unpaid and corresponding penalties for not paying on time. Don't fall into this trap. Know that with each check you receive from a client, the appropriate tax authorities will require their share. Your income is not all yours, unfortunately. (See Chapter 4 for a discussion of quarterly estimated tax payments.)

TIP!

Tax matters are best left to tax professionals. Always consult your accountant when tax-related questions and issues arise. Do not wait and hope that any tax problems you may have will somehow vanish on their own. Let your accountant handle all tax-related concerns pertaining to your business.

Chart a Course for Success

Throughout the years of running your own editorial consulting business, keep reminding yourself of these three key principles: 1) do meticulous work, 2) stay in touch with and serve your clients to their utmost satisfaction, and 3) pay your taxes on time. Always strive to do the best editorial job possible, while remaining conscientious of your clients' needs and deadlines—and while staying alert to your own business' needs—and your business will stay steadily on course through the years ahead.

Following all of the seven steps discussed in this book is what helped me start and run a successful editorial consulting business for a decade, and, I hope, for more decades to come. I have not worked in the 9-to-5 realm for more than 10 years, and

I have no intention of returning to or following that path again. I hope the seven steps discussed in this book prove useful and inspirational to you as you plan, start, and run your business each day. Consult this book often, review the case examples, and feel confident in your decision to leave full-time editorial employment behind. Exciting opportunities await you if you are open to them and ready to meet the challenges that they present.

No one can guarantee a smooth road to your success as an editorial consultant but you. By using the information in this book and proceeding systematically through each of the seven steps, you will have a firm foundation on which to base your business' start-up and development in the years ahead. Your business may experience fits and starts, and, inevitably, you are bound to make a few mistakes along the way. No one's perfect—not even an editor. Think of these "mistakes" as learning experiences, your training ground for decision making that will help you move smoothly through a maze of challenges and allow you to pursue opportunities for growth—not only the growth of your business but growth in your professionalism as well.

Afterword

*B*eing an independent editorial consultant at times can seem a thankless job, one that you toil over relentlessly while remaining anonymous and receiving few words of thanks and recognition. Remember, the day will come when a client or author praises you for a job well done and requests only you to edit his or her next assignment or book. Or, perhaps an author will show appreciation for your editorial talents by acknowledging you, by name, in the front matter of his or her book. These gestures will let you know that your services and talents are valuable, and you can feel confident in that knowledge.

I wish you much joy and success in the years ahead as you follow your dreams and begin developing your own home-based editorial consulting business. Being on your own as a self-employed individual can seem an immense and frightening undertaking because of all the unknowns that await you. On the contrary, the effort can be one of the most rewarding experiences of your life; the unknowns can metamorphose into the most wonderful opportunities. Have faith in yourself and your abilities. Always strive to do your best as an editor and business owner, and your business will thrive. As American physicist Edward Teller once said, "When you come to the end of all the light you know, and it's time to step into the darkness of the unknown, faith is knowing that one of two things shall happen: either you will be given something solid to stand on or you will be taught to fly."

Suggested Readings

Edwards P, Edwards S: The Best Home Businesses for the 21st Century, 3rd Revised Edition. New York, Jeremy Tarcher, 1999

Fife B: Make Money Reading Books: How to Start and Operate Your Own Home-Based Freelance Reading Service, 2nd Edition. Colorado Springs, CO, Piccadilly Books, 1996

Hodges JC, Whitten ME: Harbrace College Handbook, 10th Edition. San Diego, CA, Harcourt Brace Jovanovich, 1986

Holm KC (ed): Writer's Market. Cincinnati, OH, Writer's Digest Books, 2000

Holtz HR: How to Start and Run a Writing and Editing Business. New York, John Wiley & Sons, 1992

Huff PY: 101 Best Home-Based Businesses for Women. Rocklin, CA, Prima Publishing, 1995

Judd K: Copyediting: A Practical Guide, 2nd Edition. Menlo Park, CA, Crisp Publications, 1992

Kamoroff BB: Small-Time Operator: How to Start Your Own Small Business, Keep Your Books, Pay Your Taxes, and Stay Out of Trouble. Willits, CA, Bell Springs Publishing, 2000

Kopelman A (ed): National Writers Union Guide to Freelance Rates and Standard Practice. New York, National Writers Union, 1995

Neff GT, Biederman R (eds): The Writer's Essential Desk Reference, 2nd Edition. Cincinnati, OH, Writer's Digest Books, 1996

Oberlin LH: Working at Home While the Kids Are There, Too. Franklin Lakes, NJ, Career Press, 1997

Parlapiano EH, Cobe P: Mompreneurs: A Mother's Practical Step-by-Step Guide to Work-at-Home Success. New York, Berkley Publishing Group, 1996

Plotnik A: The Elements of Editing: A Modern Guide for Editors and Journalists, 32nd Edition. New York, Macmillan, 1996

Rogers T: Editorial Freelancing: A Practical Guide. Bayside, NY, Aletheia Publications, 1995

Stoughton M: Substance and Style: Instruction and Practice in Copyediting, 2nd Revised Edition. Alexandria, VA, Editorial Experts, 1996

Strunk WI Jr, White EB: Elements of Style, 3rd Edition. New York, Macmillan, 1978

Werksma LN: How to Open and Operate a Home-Based Communications Business. Old Saybrook, CT, The Globe Pequot Press, 1995

Appendix A

Marketing Packet

Jane M. Frutchey, M.S.
Editorial Consultant
Frutchey Publishing Services

1111 Country Rd. ♦ Anytown, US 00112
Phone (555) 555-5555 ♦ Fax (555) 555-5555
Email fps@you.com

Fig 1. Business card sample

Frutchey Publishing Services

♦
♦
♦

Professional Editorial Services to Meet Your Needs

1111 Country Road
Anytown, US 00112

Jane M. Frutchey, M.S.
Editorial Consultant
Frutchey Publishing Services
1111 Country Road
Anytown, US 00112
Phone (555) 555-5555
Fax (555) 555-5555
Email fps@you.com

Areas of Specialization

Frutchey Publishing Services specializes in the following services to help meet clients' individual editorial needs:

- Copyediting
- Fact-checking
- Literature searches
- Manuscript analysis and evaluation
- Proofreading
- Research/interviews
- Scholarly works editing
- Special assignment writing

♦

Fig 2a. Trifold brochure sample, outside

About the Company

Frutchey Publishing Services was established in 1990 as a one-person editorial consulting firm. The company is now expanding and provides a full range of professional editorial services to publishers of books and journals, as well as to corporate clients.

The company is owned and operated by Jane M. Frutchey, M.S., Editorial Consultant, who has more than 15 years' experience as a writer/editor.

Ready to Meet Your Needs

If you are a publisher of scholarly books and journals, corporate communications, or periodicals, Frutchey Publishing Services can help with your next editorial project. And, if you should become short-staffed as crucial editorial deadlines approach, we can provide temporary on-site services with proper advance notice.

Clients Served

Frutchey Publishing Services has assisted a wide variety of publishers and corporate clients, including the following:

- American Psychiatric Press
- Aspen Publishers
- Harcourt-Brace
- McGraw-Hill
- Monotype Composition
- Mosby-Year Book
- Saunders
- Thieme

- AAA-Maryland
- Johns Hopkins Bayview Medical Center
- Marriott International
- Maryland Hospital Association
- State Employees Federal Credit Union of Maryland
- W.B. Doner

Now Accepting Assignments

Frutchey Publishing Services is now accepting editorial assignments for the months ahead. Call (555) 555-5555 to discuss your editorial needs and to schedule your next project. Our competitive rates vary according to services provided.

Fig 2b. Trifold brochure sample, inside

Frutchey Publishing Services

1111 Country Road ♦ Anytown, US 00112
Phone (555) 555-5555 ♦ Fax (555) 555-5555 ♦ Email fps@you.com

Professional Editorial Services to Meet Your Needs

♦Areas of Specialization

Scholarly books and journals ♦ Corporate Communications ♦ Periodicals

♦Services

Copyediting
Fact-checking
Manuscript review/critique
Publications coordinating
Research
Writing

♦Publications

Books and journals
Collateral advertising materials
Manuals
Newsletters
Newspapers, magazines
Press releases
Proposals
Reports

Now Accepting and Scheduling Assignments for 2001

Call 555-555-5555 for rates and to schedule your next editorial assignment.

♦ Temporary on-site services are also available. ♦

Fig 3. Flier sample

Jane M. Frutchey
Editorial Consultant
♦♦♦
Frutchey Publishing Services
1111 Country Road ♦ Anytown, US 00112
Phone (555) 555-5555 ♦ Fax (555) 555-5555 ♦ Email fps@you.com

♦ AREAS OF SPECIALIZATION

- Copyediting, proofreading, and fact-checking services for publishers of scholarly books and journals.
- Writing, editing, and publications coordinating services for the purposes of public relations, marketing, employee, and other corporate communications.
- Researching and special assignment writing.

♦ EXPERIENCE

September 1990 - Present
Editorial Consultant
Copyediting, proofreading, and fact-checking book and journal manuscripts; researching, writing, editing, and coordinating corporate publications for the purposes of public relations, marketing, and employee communications; researching and writing news and features for local publications. Clients served include the following: AAA-Maryland, American Psychiatric Press, Aspen Publishers, Baltimore County Employees Federal Credit Union, Barry Blau & Partners, Development Design Group, Harcourt-Brace, *Harford Business Ledger*, Johns Hopkins Bayview Medical Center, Lovell-Regency Sales Corporation, Marriott International, Maryland Hospital Association, McGraw-Hill, Monotype Composition Company, Mosby-Year Book, Reese Press, Saunders, State Employees Federal Credit Union of Maryland, Thieme, *Valley Times*, W.B. Doner.

March 1990 - September 1990
Writer/Editor, Martin Marietta Aero & Naval Systems
Coordinating, editing, and proofreading corporate slide presentations and briefing materials; editing research and technical reports; providing writing and editorial support, as needed, for divisions within Aero & Naval Systems, as well as for corporate headquarters in Bethesda.

April 1988 - December 1989
Writer/Editor, Philip Willen Associates
Coordinating newsletters targeted to employees of local hospitals and health care facilities and to their community members: researching, reporting, writing, editing, managing contributing writers, arranging photo shoots, proofreading, and designing preliminary layouts; writing feature articles and story outlines for the media; writing press releases, fact sheets, public service announcements, brochures, and ad copy; assisting with special events, as necessary.

May 1987 - April 1988
Marketing Assistant, Aberdeen Proving Ground Federal Credit Union
Coordinating newsletters targeted to credit union employees and members:

- continued -

Fig 4a. Resumé sample, first page

Jane M. Frutchey
Editorial Consultant

-continued-

researching, reporting, writing, editing, proofreading, photography, and layout; writing, editing, and proofreading annual reports, brochures, press releases, ad copy, and collateral materials; planning and assisting with special events.

June 1986 - May 1987
Public Affairs Specialist, American Automobile Association of Maryland
Assisting with membership newsletter, including researching, reporting, writing, editing, arranging photo shoots, and proofreading; writing, editing, and proofreading press releases, brochures, ad copy, and collateral materials; disseminating information to the media and general public; public speaking as AAA's traffic safety representative and liaison for community and special interest groups; coordinating special events/promotions for employees, members, and the general public; conducting and tabulating surveys; researching and responding to inquiries and complaints of members and the general public; handling administrative duties.

September 1984 - June 1986
Correspondence Analyst, Blue Cross & Blue Shield of Maryland, Medicare Services
Researching, examining, evaluating, and adjusting health insurance claims; researching and analyzing physicians' reports and guidelines established by the Health Care Financing Administration; accessing and researching health insurance data bases; disseminating guidelines and health care information via correspondence to physicians and beneficiaries.

◆ **EDUCATION**
Master of Science, Professional Writing, concentration in Writing for the Public and Private Sectors, Towson University, January 1993, cumulative grade point average: 3.75.

Bachelor of Science, Mass Communication, concentration in Journalism and Public Relations, Towson University, June 1984, Magna Cum Laude, cumulative grade point average: 3.73.

◆ **INTERNSHIPS**
Harborplace Management, Winter Session 1984, Public Relations Intern.
American Automobile Association, Spring Session 1984, Public Affairs Intern.
Baltimore Magazine, Spring Session 1983, Journalism Intern.

◆ **PROFESSIONAL ORGANIZATIONS**
Baltimore Writers' Alliance
Mid-Atlantic Publishers Association

◆ **REFERENCES**
All references will be furnished upon request.

Fig 4b. Resumé sample, second page

Appendix B

Resources for Editors

Books

Altbach PG, Hoshino ES (eds): International Book Publishing: An Encyclopedia. New York, Garland Publishing, 1995

Anderson LK: Handbook for Proofreading. Lincolnwood, IL, National Textbook Company, 1990

Bernstein TM: The Careful Writer: A Modern Guide to English Usage. New York, Atheneum, 1965

Bruno MH (ed): Pocket Pal: A Graphic Arts Production Handbook, 18th Edition. Memphis, TN, Inernational Paper Company, 2000

Butcher JM: Copy-Editing: The Cambridge Handbook. Cambridge, England, Cambridge University Press, 1975

The Chicago Manual of Style: The Essential Guide for Writers, Editors, and Publishers, 14th Edition. Chicago, University of Chicago Press, 1993

Einsohn A: The Copyeditor's Handbook: A Guide for Book Publishing and Corporate Communications: With Exercises and Answer Keys. Berkeley, University of California Press, 2000

Encyclopedia of Associations, Detroit, MI, Gale Research, 1996

Fargis P, Bykofsky S (eds): The New York Public Library Desk Reference, 2nd Edition. New York, Prentice Hall, 1993

Goldstein N (ed): The Associated Press Stylebook and Libel Manual. New York, Perseus Press, 1998

Gross G (ed): Editors on Editing: What Writers Need to Know about What Editors Do. New York, Grove Press, 1993

Herman J: Writer's Guide to Book Editors, Publishers, and Literary Agents. Rocklin, CA, Prima Publishing, 1997

Li X, Crane N: Electronic Styles: A Handbook for Citing Electronic Information, 2nd Edition. Medford, NJ, Information Today, 1996

Literary Market Place. New York, Bowker, annual

Luey B: Handbook for Academic Authors. New York, Cambridge University Press, 1995

McCutcheon M: Roget's Superthesaurus, 2nd Edition. Cincinnati, OH, Writer's Digest Books, 1998

McVay BL: Getting Started in Federal Contracting: A Guide Through the Federal Procurement Maze. Burke, VA, Panoptic Enterprises, 1996

Merriam-Webster's Collegiate Dictionary, 10th Edition. Springfield, MA, 1996

Metter E: Facts in a Flash: A Research Guide for Writers. Cincinnati, OH, Writer's Digest Books, 1999

Miller C, Swift K: The Handbook of Nonsexist Writing. New York, Lippincott & Crowell, 1980

O'Neill CL, Ruder A: The Complete Guide to Editorial Freelancing. New York, Barnes & Noble, 1979

Skillin ME, Gay RM: Words into Type, 3rd Edition. Englewood Cliffs, NJ, Prentice-Hall, 1974

Stainton EM: The Fine Art of Copyediting. New York, Columbia University Press, 1991

Trade Shows Worldwide. Detroit, MI, Gale Research, 2000

Walker J, Taylor TW: The Columbia Guide to Online Style. New York, Columbia University Press, 1998

World Almanac and Book of Facts. New York, Newspaper Enterprise Association, annual

Zinsser W: On Writing Well: An Informal Guide to Writing Nonfiction, 2nd Edition. New York, Harper & Row, 1980

Grammar Hotlines

Amarillo College Grammarphone
Amarillo, TX
806-374-4726
<http://www.gabiscott.com/bigdog/index.htm>

Perdue University Grammar Hotline
West Lafayette, IN
317-494-3723
<http://www.owl.english.perdue.edu>

Portland State University Writing Helpline
Portland, OR
503-725-3570
<http://www.writingcenter.pdx.edu>

Tidewater Community College Grammar Hotline
Virginia Beach, VA
757-427-7170
<http://www.tc.cc.va.us/writcent>

University of Kansas Writer's Roost
Lawrence, KS
785-864-2399
<http://www.ukans.edu/~writing>

University of Maryland Baltimore County Grammar Hotline
Baltimore, MD
410-455-6304
<http://www.umbc7.umbc.edu/~lharris/index.html>

Whatcom Community College Writing Center
Bellingham, WA
360-676-2170
<http://www.writing.whatcom.ctc.edu>

Periodicals

American Journalism Review
1117 Journalism Building
University of Maryland, College Park
College Park, MD 20742
301-405-8803
<http://www.ajr.newslink.org>

Copy Editor
McMurry Newsletters
McMurry Campus Center
1010 E. Missouri Ave.
Phoenix, AZ 85014
602-395-5850
<http://www.mcmurry.com>

The Editorial Eye
Editorial Experts, Inc.
66 Canal Center Plaza, Suite #200
Alexandria, VA 22314
800-683-8380; 703-683-0683
<http://www.eeicommunications.com/eye>

Library Journal
245 West 17th Street
New York, NY 10011
212-463-6819
<http://www.libraryjournal.reviewsnews.com>

Publications Management
McMurry Newsletters
McMurry Campus Center
1010 E. Missouri Ave.
Phoenix, AZ 85014
602-395-5850
<http://www.mcmurry.com>

Publishers Weekly
249 West 17th Street
New York, NY 10011
212-463-6758
<http://www.publishersweekly.reviewsnews.com>

Publishing Research Quarterly
Rutgers University
Building 4051
New Brunswick, NJ 08903
908-445-2280
<http://www.transactionpub.com>

Professional Organizations

American Copy Editors Society
3 Healy Street
Huntington, NY 11743
800-393-7681
<http://www.copydesk.org>

The Association for Women in Communications
780 Ritchie Highway, Suite #28-S
Severna Park, MD 21146
410-544-7442
<http://www.womcom.org>

Council of Science Editors
11250 Roger Bacon Drive, Suite #8
Reston, VA 21090
703-437-4377
<http://councilscienceeditors.org>

Editorial Freelancers Association
71 West 23rd Street, Suite #1910
New York, NY 10010
212-929-5400
<http://www.the-efa.org>

International Association of Business Communicators
One Hallidie Plaza, Suite #600
San Francisco, CA 94102
415-544-4700; 800-776-4222
<http://www.iabc.com>

International Women's Writing Guild
P.O. Box 810, Gracie Station
New York, NY 10028
212-737-7536
<http://www.iwwg.com>

PEN (Poets, Playwrights, Editors, Essayists, Novelists) American Center
568 Broadway
New York, NY 10012
212-334-1660
<http://www.pen.org>

Teachers and Writers Collaborative
5 Union Square West
New York, NY 10003
212-691-6590
<http://www.twc.org>

Websites

<http://www.allfree.server101.com>
A site for all types of freelancers, with helpful articles, job site links, and other resources.

<http://www.bartleby.com/141>
Read full on-line text of Strunk and White's *The Elements of Style.*

<http://www.copyeditor.com>
Site of the bimonthly newsletter *Copy Editor,* which keeps editors apprised of developments in language usage and style. A searchable list of editorial jobs is included.

<http://www.elance.com>
A subscriber service that allows freelancers to profile their professional services on-line and to bid on jobs worldwide.

<http://www.freelance.com>
An on-line directory and list of resources for freelancers in the field of communications, including writers, editors, and graphics professionals.

<http://www.m-w.com>
Searchable *Merriam-Webster's Collegiate Dictionary, 10th Edition.*

<http://www.nyu.edu/classes/copyXediting/eresources.html>
New York University's list of electronic resources for copyeditors, including links to pertinent sites for editorial associations, jobs, reference works, and language usage.

<http://www.poynter.org>
A list of useful links to websites of interest to journalists and copyeditors, compiled by the Poynter Institute, St. Petersburg, Florida.

<http://www.press.uchicago.edu/misc/chicago/cmosfaq.html>
The University of Chicago Press' site for frequently asked questions regarding *The Chicago Manual of Style*, with important links to editing classes, grammar sites, and resources for electronic style guidelines.

<http://www.pubmgmt.com>
Site of the monthly newsletter *Publications Management,* with links to other websites of interest to professionals in corporate and custom publications management.

<http://www.theslot.com>
Good general interest site for copyeditors to visit.

<http://www.webgrammar.com/fft1299xtra.html>
E-zine, newsletter, tips, and references for writers, editors, researchers, educators, and web developers. A good site to investigate when pesky grammar-related dilemmas arise.

Index

Advantages of self-employment 18–21
Advertisements, paid 104–107
    fliers 105
    trade shows 105
    websites 105–107
Agreements, verbal 110
The American Medical Association Manual of Style 12, 70, 98
Arbitration 39
Associated Press Stylebook and Libel Manual 12, 70
Association for Women in Communications 37, 137
Audits 46, 52, 118
    see also Internal Revenue Service

Bank accounts, business 47–48
Book publishers, as clients 4, 11–13, 79, 96, 98, 115
    see also Clients
Bureau of Labor Statistics xv, xvi
Burnout 82, 86–90
    see also Stress
Business expenses and income, tracking 46, 48–49, 50, 51
    see also Recordkeeping
Business start-up 1–2, 4–6, 17, 21, 29–31, 37, 47, 55, 90
    expenses and financing 71–72
    and free advice from other consultants 29–30, 33–35
    how-to courses or seminars 29–33, 39, 45
    research 1, 16–17

Certified Public Accountant, need for a 45–53, 119
Chamber of Commerce 29, 31–32, 34, 37, 107, 109, 111
The Chicago Manual of Style 12, 13, 69, 98, 131, 140
Childcare needs 64
Clients 3, 4, 5, 6, 8, 11, 15, 21, 22–23, 78–79, 91–111, 114–118
    and conflicting obligations 56, 82–83
    corporate 12, 23, 57, 58, 79, 89, 96, 97, 98, 102, 110, 115
    former employers as 91–93
    individual authors as 23, 26, 79, 114–115, 116, 121
    multiple obligations to 56, 82–83, 86–87, 117

·141·   [Clients continued...]

    nonpaying 39, 78–79
    nonprofit 57, 58, 95, 96, 115
    and on-site work 83–86
    publishing 4, 12, 57, 61, 85–86, 89, 96, 98–99, 102, 111, 115
    staying in touch with 117–118
Cold telephone calls 91, 95–97
Computer problems 73–78
    fatal error 74–75
    printer 77–78
    virus 76–77
Contacts 15, 24, 32, 38, 39, 62, 91, 93, 95, 96, 97, 103, 109
    see also Networking
    colleagues and supervisors 34, 91–93, 107
    consultants and freelancers 29, 33–35, 57, 87, 96, 106
Continuing education 29, 33, 39, 113
Copyediting 114, 123

Deadlines, multiple 3, 87
Diagramming sentences 8, 10–11
Disadvantages of self-employment 21–25

E-books 12
E-zines 12, 17
Editorial Freelancers Association xv, 37, 56–57, 103, 137
Editorial guidelines, observing 12, 13, 98, 114–116
Education, editorial consultant's 1, 4–5, 19, 29, 33, 39, 102, 113, 117
Edwards, Paul and Sarah xv, 94, 123
Electronic Styles: A Handbook for Citing Electronic Information 12, 69, 132
The Elements of Editing 114, 124
Experience and skills, editorial consultant's 1, 4–11, 83, 95, 98–99, 114, 117
Expositions 33, 41, 105

Fees, setting 56–61, 80–81
    see also Hourly rate
    resources for 35, 56–57, 59–60
Full-time job, best time to leave 1, 14–15
Furniture, equipment, and supplies 65–71

Government Printing Office Style Manual 12, 70, 98
Grammar Smart 11, 70

Harbrace College Handbook 11, 70, 123
Hourly rate, determining 56–61, 80–81, 85, 86
    see also Fees

In-house style guidelines 13
Internal Revenue Service 22, 49, 50, 52, 53, 118

Job hotlines 38–39
Judd, Karen 114, 123

Language skills, editorial consultant's 7, 8, 9–11
Literary Market Place 37, 104, 132

Managing editor, working with a 61, 96, 98–99, 115–116
Marketing packet 21, 91, 96, 97, 99–102, 103, 125–129
    example of editorial consultant's 125–129
    preparing a simple, informative 99–102
Membership directory 34, 38, 103–104
Meticulous editing 10, 94, 95, 113–117, 119

National Association of Home-Based Businesses 32–33
Networking 29, 32, 33, 34, 39, 91, 107

On-line database 103
Opportunities, editorial xvi–xviii, 34, 58, 62, 83–86, 93–94, 103, 120
    business communications xvi
    health care xvi–xvii
    law xvii
    on-site xvii, 38, 83–86, 89, 92, 93, 94, 117
    technical or multimedia xvii

Paperwork, handling tax-related 46, 51–53
Plotnik, Arthur 114, 124
Pro bono work 62–63, 95
Pro-Net 103
Professional organizations 19, 34, 37–44, 57, 69, 91, 102, 103, 104, 106, 109, 111, 137–138
    benefits to joining 38–40
    questions to ask when evaluating 40–42
    caveats to joining 43–44
Proposals 22, 68, 110
Publication Manual of the American Psychological Association 12, 70
Publicity, free 107–110
    newspaper, television, radio 107–108
    workshops and speaking engagements 108–109
    writing articles 109–110

Quicken 49, 66

Recordkeeping 30, 48–49, 52
Reference books 11, 12, 13, 69–71
Resume, consultant's 21, 68, 83, 98, 99, 102, 129–130
Rush assignments 56, 79–82

Scientific Style and Format: The Council of Biology Editors Manual for Authors, Editors, and Publishers 12, 70
Service Corps of Retired Executives (SCORE) 30–31
Self-employment 1–2, 18–25, 27, 29, 34, 49, 52, 64, 72–73, 94, 121
    advantages 18–21
    disadvantages 21–25
    personality traits for 1, 2–4
Small Business Administration 29, 30–31, 37, 45, 71, 103, 118
Stress 56, 79, 82, 87, 90
    see also Burnout
Stylebooks 12–13, 69–70, 98, 114
Style sheet 14, 115

Taxes, quarterly estimated 22, 46, 49–51, 119
Tests, copyediting and proofreading 98–99

A Uniform System of Citation 12, 70

Virus, computer 76–77
    see also Computer problems
Virus-scanning software 66, 77

Webster's Collegiate Dictionary 13, 70, 133, 139
    and preferred spellings 13
Word-of-mouth referrals 94–95, 100
Work space, establishing a 63–64
Writer's Market 56, 59, 111, 123

Zip drive 66, 75

Feedback or Questions

*I*n an effort to make subsequent editions of this book as helpful as possible to self-employed editorial consultants, the author would like to hear from you. If after reading this book you have comments or suggestions about topics or additional information you would like to see included in subsequent editions, please let the author know. You also may contact the author with questions you have concerning editorial consulting. Please e-mail your feedback or questions to wjfrutchey@aol.com.